Contents

The World's Finest Assassin
Gets Reincarnated in Another World as an Aristocrat

- Prologue — The Assassin Is Invited to the Sanctuary ...001
- Chapter 1 — The Assassin Finds Unexpected Company ...011
- Chapter 2 — The Assassin Negotiates ...023
- Chapter 3 — The Assassin Receives a Party Invitation ...031
- Chapter 4 — The Assassin Gives Warning ...037
- Chapter 5 — The Assassin Makes a Wager ...043
- Chapter 6 — The Assassin Gives His Consent ...053
- Chapter 7 — The Assassin Has a Clandestine Meeting ...059
- Chapter 8 — The Assassin Receives a Job ...071
- Chapter 9 — The Assassin Shares a Secret ...079
- Chapter 10 — The Assassin Learns Dia's Skills ...087
- Chapter 11 — The Assassin Learns Tarte's Skills ...095
- Chapter 12 — The Assassin's Chocolate ...105
- Chapter 13 — The Assassin Sets Out ...115
- Chapter 14 — The Assassin Is Tested ...123
- Chapter 15 — The Assassin Gains a New Ally ...133
- Chapter 16 — The Assassin Kills a Prince ...143
- Chapter 17 — The Assassin Goes on a Date with His Little Sister ...155
- Chapter 18 — The Assassin Keeps an Ally in Check ...165
- Chapter 19 — The Assassin Shares His Plan ...175
- Chapter 20 — The Assassin Takes Consideration ...185
- Chapter 21 — The Assassin Takes Up Arms ...195
- Chapter 22 — The Assassin Sets a Trap ...205
- Chapter 23 — The Assassin Challenges the Beast God ...213
- Chapter 24 — The Assassin Is Reunited with a Friend ...223
- Chapter 25 — The Assassin Fights with His Friend ...235
- Epilogue — The Assassin Sees Off His Friend ...243
- Afterword ...251

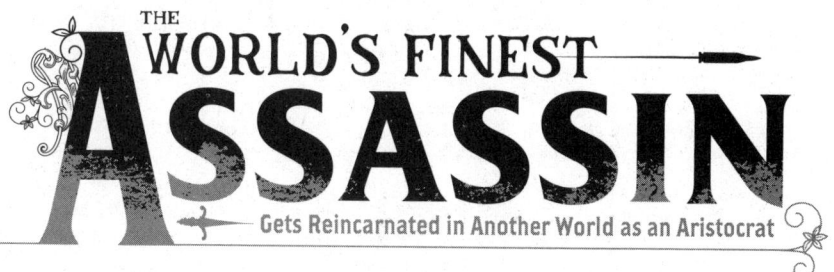

4

Rui Tsukiyo

Illustration by Reia

New York

The World's Finest Assassin Gets Reincarnated in Another World as an Aristocrat, Vol. 4
Rui Tsukiyo

Translation by Luke Hutton
Cover art by Reia

This book is a work of fiction. Names, characters, places, and incidents are the product of the author's imagination or are used fictitiously. Any resemblance to actual events, locales, or persons, living or dead, is coincidental.

SEKAI SAIKO NO ANSATSUSHA, ISEKAI KIZOKU NI TENSEI SURU Vol. 4
©Rui Tsukiyo, Reia 2020
First published in Japan in 2020 by KADOKAWA CORPORATION, Tokyo.
English translation rights arranged with KADOKAWA CORPORATION, Tokyo through TUTTLE-MORI AGENCY, INC., Tokyo.

English translation © 2022 by Yen Press, LLC

Yen Press, LLC supports the right to free expression and the value of copyright. The purpose of copyright is to encourage writers and artists to produce the creative works that enrich our culture.

The scanning, uploading, and distribution of this book without permission is a theft of the author's intellectual property. If you would like permission to use material from the book (other than for review purposes), please contact the publisher. Thank you for your support of the author's rights.

Yen On
150 West 30th Street, 19th Floor
New York, NY 10001

Visit us at yenpress.com
facebook.com/yenpress
twitter.com/yenpress
yenpress.tumblr.com
instagram.com/yenpress

First Yen On Edition: February 2022

Yen On is an imprint of Yen Press, LLC.
The Yen On name and logo are trademarks of Yen Press, LLC.

The publisher is not responsible for websites (or their content) that are not owned by the publisher.

Library of Congress Cataloging-in-Publication Data
Names: Tsukiyo, Rui, author. | Reia, 1990– illustrator.
Title: The world's finest assassin gets reincarnated in another world / Rui Tsukiyo ; illustration by Reia.
Other titles: Sekai saikou no ansatsusha, isekai kizoku ni tensei suru. English
Description: First Yen On edition. | New York : Yen On, 2020–
Identifiers: LCCN 2020043584 | ISBN 9781975312411 (v. 1 ; trade paperback) | ISBN 9781975312435 (v. 2 ; trade paperback) | ISBN 9781975333355 (v. 3 ; trade paperback) | ISBN 9781975334574 (v. 4 ; trade paperback)
Subjects: LCSH: Assassins—Fiction. | GSAFD: Fantasy fiction.
Classification: LCC PL876.S858 S4513 2020 | DDC 895.6/36—dc23
LC record available at https://lccn.loc.gov/2020043584

ISBNs: 978-1-9753-3457-4 (paperback)
       978-1-9753-3458-1 (ebook)

10 9 8 7 6 5 4 3 2 1

LSC-C

Printed in the United States of America

Prologue: The Assassin Is Invited to the Sanctuary

We were on our way to the royal capital after defeating the beetle demon. Our conveyance was a carriage pulled by a rhinoceros monster, whose strength and stamina far outpaced normal animals.

"I am impressed you were able to tame such a powerful monster, sir," I said to Marquis Granvallen, who was sitting next to me. I spoke to him politely because he was older and of a higher position than me.

"It was quite a challenge. My domain has been performing research on domesticating monsters for decades, and we only recently achieved actual results."

It made sense that knowledge on domesticating monsters would be scarce.

Monsters always increased in number when the Demon King appeared, but they never truly vanished. They had mana, making them tougher than regular beasts. There had always been those who wanted to tame them, but their violent nature made progress on that front difficult.

"Have you domesticated other types of monsters as well?" I questioned.

"No, only rhinoceroses. Every monster is different. These are enough for me. They are very useful on the battlefield as well."

"I can imagine. I would definitely not want to meet such a creature in combat."

The rhinoceros's skin was so thick that it wouldn't even feel an arrow or spear. If multiple of them charged as a group, they would probably break an army's line of defense.

"I believe the monster manipulation arts of House Granvallen to be every bit as valuable as the medical arts of House Tuatha Dé," Marquis Granvallen boasted.

"I agree with you," I answered.

All right, that's enough small talk. I might need to make some preparations before we reach the royal castle. I need information.

"Marquis Granvallen, you stated earlier that preparations are being carried out at the royal castle to celebrate our victory over the demon. Have specific plans been set in place for after we arrive?"

"That's right. It was hastily decided that a party should be held as soon as news of your feat reached the castle. The plan is to hold it in four days. That is why my help was requested. The Alam Karla even said she wishes to invite you to the Sanctuary."

Reaching the palace in four days by horse-drawn carriage was unlikely. That was why Marquis Granvallen's services were needed.

The thing that worried me was the celebration. There was no way anyone should have so easily believed we defeated a demon.

And what was that he said about the Sanctuary and the Alam Karla?

The Alam Karla was a person of high standing.

"Why did the central government believe my report? I don't know why they would trust that someone other than the hero was able to defeat a demon," I asked.

"I know nothing of that. I was only told to transport the Holy Knight to the capital, Sir Lugh," replied the marquis.

"I see. Then, do you mind my asking if you believe my report?"

"Of course I believe you... We are allies, after all."

"Allies?"

Marquis Granvallen smiled suggestively and whispered in my ear, "I also endorse Naoise's ambitions."

Naoise was a son of one of the four major dukedoms and a classmate of mine. He aspired to change the country. I had known Naoise was gathering allies at the Royal Academy, but I couldn't believe he was able to win over someone like Marquis Granvallen.

After that, I continued to probe the marquis. I couldn't be certain of anything, but I gathered a significant amount of intelligence.

The journey would've taken five days by horse, but we arrived in a day and a half.

Our carriage passed by the Royal Academy on the outskirts of the capital along the way. The reconstruction was progressing swiftly.

We entered the city and proceeded to the castle.

I was given ceremonial attire and told to change. The clothes were a good deal more elegant than our academy uniforms and designed with a knight motif.

Dia and Tarte were also handed formal garments, although theirs looked different from mine. Because I had been dubbed a Holy Knight, Dia and Tarte were now recognized as my attendants.

"Lord Lugh, you look so handsome in that outfit," Tarte commented.

"Yeah, it suits you perfectly... I don't think this looks great on me, though. Classy clothes like this just don't work on short people," Dia lamented.

"...I don't feel very sure of myself in this outfit, either. It's a little tight on my chest, too. I prefer lighter clothing," added Tarte. She looked like she was having trouble breathing. I decided it would be best not to ask why. Dia was looking at her resentfully, and I pretended not to notice that as well.

"I think you both look great," I stated.

It was a nice change seeing them both in masculine clothing.

It would look better on Maha, though.

"Hearing you say that makes me feel better," responded Dia.

"Yes, I'll do my best to bear it," Tarte declared.

"I'm glad. Let's get going," I said.

The servants were looking restless. They had probably been told to hurry things along.

Marquis Granvallen informed us that the Alam Karla awaited our arrival in the Sanctuary.

The Alam Karla was not an individual's name but rather an inherited title belonging to the highest-ranking shrine maiden of Alamism, the national religion.

A servant led Tarte, Dia, and me through a hidden passage in the castle into a chamber with a mystical atmosphere. Stained glass windows had been set into the walls, a rarity in this world, and antique prickets held candles that illuminated them. One thing bothered me about the room, however. There was some manner of power that I could only describe as black light obstructing some sections of the walls.

So this is the Sanctuary.

"Wow, it's so beautiful," praised Dia.

"Yes, it's making me feel a little tense," Tarte admitted.

Their eyes darted around the chamber in wonder. They hadn't yet noticed the strangeness of this place. The exquisite furnishings had them spellbound, and rightfully so, for each piece was on par with a national treasure. Before long, a few others joined us. Evidently, we were not the only ones who had been invited.

"Hey, Naoise, Epona, and Ms. Barton. Long time no see," I greeted.

"Just call me Rachel. You outrank me now that you're a Holy Knight, so there's no need to address me formally," Ms. Barton responded. The woman was tall and beautiful, and she had her hair in a ponytail. She had recently graduated from the Royal Academy at the top of her class, and she was considered the young hope of the Royal Order.

"This is an unexpected assembly," I remarked.

"I suppose you could call this the hero's party. You all were personally selected because you are familiar with Epona, close to his age, and extremely skilled. Naoise's social standing may have played a role in his selection, however," Rachel explained.

"...Are you insulting me?" responded an offended Naoise.

"I'm only speaking the truth. Personally, I'd rather tie the knot with Lugh. I never could've imagined you'd be named a Holy Knight and then immediately slay a demon. You'd be a great husband," Rachel continued, putting her arm around mine and pressing herself against me.

Dia glared, and Tarte began to tear up. Rachel assured us that it was a joke and released me.

With a strained laugh, Naoise remarked, "Just as popular as ever."

"Epona, have you heard anything about why we were summoned here so urgently?" I inquired. The hero had been trying to hide behind Rachel despite her status.

"Um, all we know is that the Alam Karla has something important to tell us," Epona answered, acting timid as usual.

Epona was a boyish girl like Rachel, but she lacked the same dignified aura, so the ceremonial attire didn't suit her as well in my eyes.

"I see, so you're in the same boat as us. How have you all been doing since the last time we met?" I asked.

"We've been fine. Nothing much has happened," replied Epona.

Everyone exchanged information and got caught up on recent events. It sounded like the hero and those with her had been charged with defending the royal capital and the surrounding area. They had been spending all of their time training.

A little while later, a girl sporting white hair, dressed in an equally pale-colored tunic, made her entrance. She was a beautiful young woman in her early twenties. She was the Alam Karla, the highest-ranking shrine maiden.

It was my first time laying eyes on her, but I knew at a glance that her look was modeled after the goddess who had sent me to this world. Her hair was not naturally white, and there was no way she had dyed it that color by coincidence.

This meant that the goddess must have, for some reason,

shown herself and interfered with this country. Perhaps she had even founded Alamism to make her managing the world easier.

"Thank you for gathering here today, those who will serve as humanity's shield." The Alam Karla spoke with a clear, well-projected voice. She had obviously been trained in public speaking to ensure her words reached the hearts of listeners.

Religion was a spiritual matter, but the means for spreading it and fostering belief were based on cold logic. The Alam Karla's behavior, vocalization, how she filled time, and more were all meticulously calculated.

"You all were invited here today so that I could share with you a secret. Bear witness to the truth, chosen ones," the Alam Karla stated. At her command, the candles were all extinguished, and darkness filled the room.

Several spots on the wall shone dimly, and the black light surrounding them vanished.

Light was flowing from statues placed at regular intervals along the walls. There were eight in total, each depicting a grotesque combination of man and animal, including a snake, a pig, and a beetle.

The pig and the beetle sculptures were a different shade than the rest. While all the others were green, they were conspicuously red.

"It can't be a coincidence," I said to myself.

There was a statue representing each of the three demons I had encountered thus far. That the pig Epona had killed and the beetle I had slain were the only red ones was not chance.

"There are eight demons in total, and two of them have already been felled. Your job is to kill the remaining six and to halt their efforts to revive the Demon King."

The government must have believed my report because these statues were linked to the lives of the demons. My account had never been necessary. They'd already known of the demon's demise.

That aside, what's this about halting the demons' efforts to revive the Demon King? Does that mean the Demon King can't return naturally and requires the demons to perform some action to bring them back to life? Why am I being told this now?

Those weren't the only questions on my mind, either.

Had I known these eight statues existed, I would have been better equipped to identify the demons. Such knowledge would have been invaluable in battle. Why were we only being given this vital information now? Making sense of it all was difficult.

The lights turned back on, and the Alam Karla stood there, smiling. Apparently, she wasn't going to volunteer anything more on her own.

Turning to face her, I spoke up.

Chapter 1 | The Assassin Finds Unexpected Company

"Your Holiness. Why was this not revealed to us sooner? If we had been allowed to view these sculptures, we would have been able to guess at which demons might appear, infer their abilities, and prepare for them," I said.

A demon's form was important. They, like monsters, possessed abilities that related to the animals they took after. That was only what we could learn from the statues alone. She undoubtedly knew more about the demons than even my Balor information network was incapable of finding.

"What you say is correct. However, the existence of this Sanctuary is top secret. We could not show you this room until there was no doubt you could be trusted," the Alam Karla responded.

Don't force me into killing demons if you don't trust me.

I took a moment to digest her words.

"If that's the case, does that mean the demons' efforts to revive the Demon King, and their means for doing so, are also secret?"

"Of course. Such things are normally only shared with the hero. If this information were to become known to the public, it would bring ruination. However, Sir Lugh, the church has decided you are worthy of being told."

That reply filled in more puzzle pieces for me, and I was quickly assembling them.

I realized I'd already stumbled upon a few clues. First, the Fruit of Life the beetle demon had tried to make. Second, the government's extreme fear that demons would attack the royal capital. Third, the state of the towns that were attacked. And fourth, the Alam Karla asserting that public knowledge of the truth would cause disaster.

When I considered all these factors, there was only one conclusion.

"The demons want to use humans to create a Fruit of Life and then use that to revive the Demon King. I'm guessing they need tens of thousands of people to create it, which makes large cities obvious targets," I said.

"That is correct. You are quite clever. The demons labor to gather mortal spirits to produce Fruits of Life. Souls have different degrees of strength. For example, the hero's soul alone would be enough to create a Fruit of Life, but fifty thousand ordinary people would be needed."

Upon hearing such a high number, everyone present except for me looked surprised.

At last, the demons' strategy made sense. Attacking a small village with a population of only a few hundred would hardly further their goal. That was why they aimed for large metropolises like Milteu, the city of commerce where I launched my cosmetic brand Natural You, and the royal capital.

What would happen if the kingdom were to share this information with the public? Towns and cities with rich economic activity would face mass depopulation as everyone left to find safety elsewhere. Major centers of industry would wither and die.

Politics and the economy would fall into turmoil, causing the country to suffer.

There was no way the citizenry could be permitted to learn that cities were the demons' targets. This was also unquestionably why the government kept the hero in the royal capital.

"I am sorry we hid this from you until now. If we had had reason to believe you are a Chosen like me…" The Alam Karla trailed off.

"A 'Chosen'?" I questioned.

"You received a vision from the great white goddess Venus, did you not? The characteristics of the deity you described in your letter are, without a doubt, the same as the Venus I see in my dreams. If she granted you a spell capable of killing demons, I have to imagine you are a Chosen, one who has received divine favor."

The Alam Karla, the highest-ranking shrine maiden, was said to be the mouthpiece of the goddess. I had figured that was nothing more than flowery language to make her seem important, but it appeared that was not the case.

The goddess came to her in dreams. That meant the Alam Karla's job was to relay the goddess's words to human society.

"I am not quite a Chosen, Your Holiness… I have only seen the goddess twice, once when I was little and again the other day when I was given the Demonkiller spell. What about you, if you don't mind my asking?" I said.

"Roughly once every three months. It is by the supreme goddess Venus's words, spoken through the Alam Karlas, that this world has flourished."

This was consistent with what I knew of the goddess. Venus could see the future, so she didn't have to rely on other supernatural abilities or miracles to bring about change. She could do it with words alone. It was a very logical method of interference that didn't require her to expend much energy.

"Your Holiness, next time you meet the goddess, please offer her my thanks. Tell her this: 'I will live up to your expectations, so please watch over me.'"

"Oh, how nice. I will pass on your message."

The undercurrent of my statement for the deity was *"I'll do what you want of me, so don't interfere."*

"Hero, Chosen, and your fellow companions. Please hear my words. Your mission is to exterminate the remaining six demons and prevent the Demon King's revival."

We all performed a typical Alamism bow.

This has been very enlightening.

The snake demon had been forthcoming with useful intelligence as well.

She detested the idea of the beetle demon being the one to produce the Fruits of Life needed for the Demon King's revival. That led me to the assumption that the demons were competing against one another, and that was something I could take advantage of.

After being reminded that we couldn't breathe a word of what we had learned there, we departed the Sanctuary.

When our group left the hidden passage and returned to the castle, Epona turned to face me. "I'm surprised they were keeping such a massive secret," she said.

"Yeah. I would have liked to know earlier, but they had their reasons not to let us know," I responded.

"Let's both do our best. We can't allow something as dangerous as the Demon King to return."

I smiled and nodded.

My mind turned to the future only I was privy to. The goddess had told me that Epona was going to go insane after killing the Demon King. That meant that in that future, the demons would succeed.

No, it's too early to give up... If the future were set in stone, there would have been no purpose in sending me to this world. I'll fight until the very end.

A party was held the next day.

It was even grander than the celebration when I had been named a Holy Knight, and the mood was noticeably different as well. Aristocrats from near and far were in great spirits.

They hadn't trusted my abilities initially. Now that I had killed a demon, I had gained their confidence. I couldn't blame them. After all, I hadn't been certain my method of demon slaying would work.

I was praised for my triumph during the festivities and formally recognized as a Chosen by the church. This would make it far easier to do as I pleased. As long as I was endeavoring to end the demon threat, very few were left in the kingdom who could challenge my actions.

Perhaps that was part of the goddess's plan. The position of the Alam Karla itself could have been created solely to proclaim me a Chosen and make my life easier.

There was one unexpected development during the party— my formula for Demonkiller was made public.

This surprised me, given the presence of foreign nobles at the party. The Demonkiller spell could have made for a strong negotiating chip, depending on how it was used.

Every power in the world would have been desperate to know the secret to killing demons without the hero. Without it, they'd be doomed the moment a demon appeared. Sharing such a valuable bit of knowledge like that for free seemed odd.

"Oh my, it seems your glass is empty, Sir Lugh," came a woman's voice.

A noblewoman with dark skin and black hair sauntered over to me, holding two cups, one of which she passed to me. Her voluptuous body was clothed in a revealing outfit.

What the heck is she doing here? What does this mean?

I took the glass while being careful not to show that I was troubled.

"Never in my wildest dreams would I have expected to see you in a place like this," I remarked.

"Why, this is the first time we've met, Sir Lugh. Perhaps you mistake me for someone else?" she responded with a giggle.

There was no way I was wrong.

This woman was the snake demon I had encountered after killing the beetle one. She had disguised herself as a human. Her mana and the miasma that accompanied demons had also been concealed.

Still, I knew.

Assassins were masters of disguise, and we also had the skill to see through the trickery of others. We could identify a person not just from their appearance, but also their smell, way of speaking, habits, timing, mannerisms, and so on.

"It seems I was. My apologies. Yet it feels like we were somehow fated to meet here. Perhaps later we should retire somewhere we might speak more freely?" I proposed.

"Are you asking me out on a date? How bold. Going out with the Holy Knight would be such an honor. See you later, then, Sir Lugh," she purred back.

That was the response I'd expected. She was clearly here for me. The snake demon curtsied and took her leave, a swarm of male nobles bustling after her. After watching her go, Dia and Tarte came up to me with plates full of food.

"I see you ogling, Lugh! She is *extremely* beautiful," said Dia.

"Um, do you like that kind of woman?" Tarte asked meekly.

It seemed like neither had figured out it was the snake demon.

"She's not necessarily my type, but I do find her a little interesting," I answered.

"Oh really? I told you I would allow unfaithfulness if it was with Tarte, but I *will* be mad if you cheat on me with a seductive older woman you just met, okay?" warned Dia.

"Lady Dia, Lord Lugh would never do something like that…," Tarte protested, jumping to my defense.

It wounded me that Dia was so quick to mistrust me, although her jealousy was cute.

"Relax. You're the one I love, Dia. I'm only interested in her for my work."

"Hmm, all right."

That's right. Work. That's why I was reborn here, and now it's my job as a Holy Knight.

I had promised to meet with the snake demon later, but she obviously intended far more than a casual encounter. I needed to know how she had wormed her way into this country and what kind of position she held.

~Goddess's Point of View~

In an alabaster room, a deity wreathed in white observed and analyzed the world, as she always did.

When the goddess was alone, she was as expressionless as a doll.

The goddess had a thousand faces, and she was able to simulate whatever personality suited her needs, taking into account the situation and the person she was speaking with. Thus, when alone, she had no need of expression and didn't bother with the effort.

Her face remained unnaturally neutral. If a human were to see her, they probably would have thought she resembled a machine.

"Progression to next phase confirmed. Deviation from estimated destruction of the world confirmed. Margin of error is 5.623. I attribute uncertain factors to Lugh Tuatha Dé. Primary causes are the subjugation of demons and alterations to the world brought about by his hand. Probability of the world's destruction lowered from 99.87 percent to 86.23 percent."

While the odds still favored the planet's annihilation, the drop was a major success.

"Deaths of Fallan Forteil, Deique Grouline, and Nacha Coradorph confirmed. Lugh Tuatha Dé is the only surviving external factor. Obtainment of resources by way of external phenomena confirmed. Use them to invite new external… No."

The goddess did not believe in anything. Probability was her only guide.

No matter what worldly resources she used in her simulations, things always fell to ruin. That was why she'd had no choice but to invite factors from the outside.

The first was Lugh Tuatha Dé, but he was not the only one.

Statistically, it was more favorable to introduce multiple individuals.

The same reasoning could be applied to taking a test. It was easy to get a seventy. Raising your score above that was where it got complicated. Aiming for a perfect score demanded more than three times the effort.

Thus, the goddess didn't bet everything on one person. Rather than attempt creating one perfect individual, she hoped to raise multiple seventies and trust that one would succeed.

That should have increased the overall chances.

"Error in guiding principles confirmed. Recognition that Lugh Tuatha Dé is special. Proposal to higher beings. Forwarding Lugh Tuatha Dé's accomplishments. Rather than bolstering the number of attempts by introducing more external factors, we should concentrate on Lugh Tuatha Dé. I have decided there is something about Lugh Tuatha Dé that probabilities cannot describe."

Even if none of her decisions until now had been incorrect by statistical theory, all external factors other than Lugh Tuatha Dé had perished without exhibiting any influence on the world.

Still, the goddess did not think her initial decision was incorrect. She possessed no attachment to her own choices, however. If something outperformed expectations, she would recognize it and adjust.

As a result of her recent analysis, she accepted that Lugh Tuatha Dé was unusual and worth taking a gamble on. For that reason, rather than use the resources they secured from the deaths of the external factors to replenish their stock, she decided to bet on Lugh Tuatha Dé.

The higher beings answered the goddess's proposal with consent.

"Approval confirmed. Additional resources for Lugh Tuatha Dé obtained. I will entrust the world to him."

She would not invite any more external factors into the world.

This would simultaneously be good news and bad news for Lugh Tuatha Dé. He would receive even more support, but everything rested on him now.

"Running simulation for optimal use of additional resources. Outcomes detected: 72,346. Among those, the highest probability is... No, probabilities are unreliable when it comes to Lugh Tuatha Dé... Focus should be placed elsewhere."

The goddess made a decision, one that ignored her calculation of the future.

"Requesting resources from higher beings... Approval received... Assets will be ready for use in thirty-seven days. Accessing channel into present world, the Alam Karla, to ensure optimal use."

Alamism. A religion to guide humanity... It sounded good when put that way, but the goddess had merely created it as a tool for managing the world at a minimal cost. She used it to speak to the shrine maiden known as the Alam Karla in her dreams.

Any action the deity took to interfere demanded resources. When she spoke directly to people in the world, she had to do so with the knowledge that it could mean her destruction.

Thankfully, appearing in the dreams of only one person cost her very little. She was able to spread the religion of Alamism throughout the world simply by talking to one girl in her dreams.

This convenient tool had not developed naturally; the goddess had created it out of necessity. With her power, it wasn't tough.

The alabaster deity smiled within the dream of the current Alam Karla. Then she began to talk about Lugh Tuatha Dé.

She filled her smile with the compassion of a saint. The goddess always wore the facade the one speaking with her desired. She understood what kind of personality one who depended on the gods wished to see.

The goddess broke off her connection to the girl and closed her eyes. It wasn't sleep, but rather a total shutdown. There was nothing left she could do. As such, the best course of action was to wait until such time that she was needed again.

Just as Alamism was her creation, so, too, was she a tool meant to manage the world.

Chapter 2 | The Assassin Negotiates

I had thought I would see the snake demon again, but I didn't know it would be so soon, and especially not at a party in the royal capital, of all places.

A demon attending a celebration in the royal capital was nothing to sneeze at. Only Alvan's best were permitted entry. If she felt like it, the demon could slaughter every member of the central government right now.

I followed one of Snake's servants down a hall flanked with rooms on loan to aristocratic guests.

All eyes turned to me as we passed by. As a Holy Knight and now also a Chosen, I was the center of attention. To add to that, I was visiting a woman's room late at night. A young, beautiful woman at that. I was sure rumors would be circulating the next day.

The servant knocked on a door, their master responded, and the entrance opened.

"Thank you very much for your invitation, Countess Granfelt," I said.

After meeting Snake at the party, I had researched what alias she was operating under.

She was Countess Granfelt, the wife of Count Granfelt. The

previous Count Granfelt was a great man, but his heir was an incompetent fool who wasted his family's fortune. He was a stereotypical ruined noble.

Half a year ago, he had married, and *she* was his wife. Count Granfelt died a month after the wedding, and she ended up in charge of the domain, improving its management dramatically in just a few months.

Her looks and her skill had earned her popularity and praise inside and outside of the domain. I was surprised that a demon could adapt so well to human society.

"I was so looking forward to your arrival, Sir Lugh. Please, come here," she called with a laugh and a smile. The sex appeal of this voluptuous woman was enough to make any man dizzy.

She was releasing pheromones just like Tarte did when she used Beastification. The concentration, however, was significantly thicker. Unlike Tarte, she was probably doing this intentionally.

Most men would be lured by the scent, sensual body, and beckoning gestures, whether they truly wished it or not. During my assassin training, I had built up a tolerance to many drugs and possessed countermeasures for the pheromones, but even I had trouble resisting her.

Any normal person would have been done for.

"I have some very nice tea," she offered.

"No, I'm fine. I'm not thirsty," I replied.

"Please, don't be so wary around me. I haven't poisoned the tea. I only want to make you welcome, love."

"Amusing."

Don't make me laugh. You're telling me not to be wary while you're trying to seduce me?

"Oh goodness, have you figured it all out already? You can

drop the act as well, then. Everyone here is on my side, after all. Show me the cold, knifelike sharpness you displayed on the battlefield. That behavior fits you so much better and really sets my heart racing."

Countess Granfelt snapped, and the servants turned into giant white serpents.

The demon's attendants had been monsters with the ability to disguise themselves. With no humans in the room, that enabled me to speak as a demon-killing assassin. I decided to oblige Snake's request.

"Try anything now, and I'll make sure you're exposed. If you plan on attacking, by all means, make your attempt," I stated.

"You are quite intelligent, so I'll refrain from doing that kind of thing," the demon answered calmly.

She understood me well.

After learning her servants were monsters, I needed to consider the possibility that there were many more of their ilk in the castle. If they so wished, they could murder countless innocents. I didn't want to see that happen.

This demon was clever. There was no room for letting my guard down while negotiating with her, but it would also save me a lot of time.

"I'm floored that a demon was able to become so impressive a noble as to be invited to the royal castle. I didn't think the fight was *this* hopeless. You can easily overhear our every move, and worst of all, the lives of very many important people are in your grasp. Just how many have you gutted? If you felt like it, you could manipulate this entire country, no?"

I was able to bear the pheromones, but I was sure most people would succumb. I didn't even want to think about how many puppets Snake had in the central government. Undoubtedly, she possessed methods beyond sex appeal to compel others to obey.

"Not that many. You were able to resist, but you would've been a luxury. I'm still hurt, though. I never thought I'd see a man unswayed by my charms," she said, snuggling against me and running a finger down my chest.

"Sorry, but I know a girl who is way more attractive than you."

"Hmm, I wonder which one it is? The silver-haired doll? The golden-haired fox pup? Both of them are so adorable. Your young love is so pure. It makes me want to tear you apart."

"If you even think about laying a hand on Dia or Tarte, I will eliminate you. You can take the entire country hostage, but I'll never allow that."

I glared at Snake with murderous intent. A normal person would have fainted under that gaze. Conversely, I could also completely disguise my intent to kill and keep a person at ease until I ended their life.

Snake's smile spasmed a little. It seemed she understood how serious I was.

"Sorry about that, love. I didn't intend to make you angry. Let's put the jokes aside and proceed with negotiations."

It looked like we were getting to the point.

Snake drew back the finger she had been tracing down my chest and backed away.

"You don't want the Demon King to be revived. Is that right?" I asked.

If Snake wanted the Demon King to return, there was no way she would have revealed her identity to me. With her political influence, she likely could have sent the hero and me far away, enabling her to claim a whole city without interference. And there was nothing stopping her from doing as much multiple times.

"I'm delighted to see you catch on so quickly. Yes, the truth is, I want the Demon King to stay dead," she confessed.

"Your reasoning?"

"When the Demon King is reborn, the demons die. I don't want to die."

"That's easy to understand. But give me more details. If that's the case, why are the other demons working to resurrect the Demon King? It doesn't make sense. Are the others suicidal?"

Snake yawned as if bored.

"At least three Fruits of Life need to be offered. The revived Demon King then absorbs all the demons. The demon who produced the most Fruits of Life becomes the base for the Demon King. If you don't want your consciousness to vanish, you have no choice but to produce more Fruits of Life than the others."

In other words, demons were nothing more than nourishment for the Demon King. They fed the Demon King the Fruits of Life and then had to sacrifice themselves, too.

"Why are you not racing against the others to produce Fruits of Life?"

"Even if I do become the base for the Demon King, will that really be me? The thought of having the other demons and the Fruits of Life…tens of thousands of human souls…poured into me makes me want to puke. I'm fine as I am. That is why I'm hindering the others."

"That's all reasonable, but wouldn't it have been easier just to convince the other demons to drop reviving the Demon King? They might be of the same mind."

"No. All those idiots think about is being the one to become the Demon King. Demons desire power by nature, and they are following that instinct. They're nothing more than animals."

"But you're different?"

"That's right. I have all the strength I need. It's actually quite fun living among humans. The management of my domain is going well, and I have as much luxury as I could want. I hold human culture in high regard. I want to continue my current life and enjoy human pleasures and pastimes to my heart's content. That is my aim, and the other demons are in my way."

One of an assassin's essential skills was mind reading. Snake was definitely telling the truth.

"Then our interests align," I said.

"Yes. That is why I revealed to you that I am a demon. The hero is too green and would be impossible to negotiate with. That little girl would be overcome by a sense of righteousness and destroy me. But you're different. All right, I just gave you a heap of information. Perhaps you should share something helpful in return?" she inquired with a giggle.

She wasn't wrong about that. I was the only one who had benefited from our exchange so far.

"You're right. Here's what I'm willing to reveal. If you don't join forces with me, the Demon King will absolutely be revived, and you will die. The goddess, or whatever she is, told me about what's to come. As things are now, the Demon King's return is guaranteed, the hero will kill them, and then she herself will go insane and destroy the world in a blind rampage... My goal is to change that future."

"Oh my. You really are a Chosen."

"That I am. I'm acting on orders from the goddess. At her instruction, I am steering the world from its fate."

Chapter 2

That was half a lie.

"Goodness me. When you put it that way, I have no choice but to cooperate with you. Hmm-hmm, how interesting. I haven't given you my name yet. Please call me Mina. Normally, I only allow my adorable little pets to address me as such, but you're a special case."

Something about the way she said *pets* made me think she actually meant *slaves*.

Mina reached out for a handshake, and I obliged.

I had acquired a good ally. She could aid me with politics in the castle and provide intel on demons.

Mina hadn't deceived me in any major ways, but she had slipped in fibs here and there. The best liars knew how to insert small lies into the truth.

I was confident she detested the idea of other demons merging with her. However, she was lying about the tens of thousands of human souls. That notion didn't appear to trouble her one bit. Furthermore, it was true that Mina was happy and would like to continue her current life, but she had lied when claiming she desired no more. Demons craved power by instinct.

That all drew me to one conclusion: Mina's goal was to become the Demon King after killing all the other demons. That way, she could ensure they would not enter her body. Her aim was to use this nation and me to that end.

It was a genuinely cunning scheme. Mina had great ambition, making her easier to trust and manipulate.

Once Mina was the only demon left, or if she reached a point where she was confident she could slay the rest of her kin, she would try to end my life. As I understood her true intentions, the temptation to assassinate her would grow as she became less valuable to me.

We were now locked in a game of trying to wring as much as we could from the other while still being the first to strike.

"That was a fruitful negotiation. How about we have sex to celebrate? I just can't help but long for intimacy in the presence of such a fine man."

"Were you not listening? I already have a girlfriend I love very much."

"You're so uptight. That's a shame. I could satisfy you in ways that puny human girl never could."

"I'm not interested. Also, as a pointer, pleasures of the body are not everything. I look for something greater in the one I love. Something I couldn't gain from you."

"Oh my, I'm so embarrassed that you said that to me with a straight face. Youth never ceases to amaze."

I took my leave. Mina would use me, and I her. I intended to get everything I could from this relationship.

I'm gonna be in trouble once I get back to the apartment.

I was sure Dia would be angry with me for visiting such a sexy woman. Tarte wouldn't voice her displeasure, but she would stare at me nonstop with those sad eyes of hers.

It was a little annoying but also proof that they cared for me. Strangely, thinking about it that way made it sound adorable.

Chapter 3: The Assassin Receives a Party Invitation

After my clandestine meeting with the snake demon Mina, I returned to the room that had been provided for Dia, Tarte, and me.

"What do you know, the cheater has returned," Dia announced.

"Welcome back, Lord Lugh," greeted Tarte.

The former looked wounded and was puffing out her cheeks, while the latter's eyes were moist from crying. My expectations had been so on the nose that I almost laughed.

Tarte took my jacket and hung it on the wall.

"I wasn't cheating on you. That was for work," I answered.

"And what kind of job has you meeting alone with a seductress like her? She was definitely interested in you. She practically looked ready to eat you," Dia fired back.

Eat me, huh...? You're not wrong.

"I need Countess Granfelt's cooperation. She can serve as a quick source of information and make it easier for me to act freely."

Dia frowned. "You're lying. Counts don't have that kind of political power."

From highest to lowest, the aristocratic hierarchy went like this: duke, margrave, marquis, count, viscount, baron, and lastly, knight. Just as Dia had stated, a count usually wouldn't possess that much influence.

"Even if she doesn't hold much sway herself, the men she has ensnared do. I wonder just how many in the central government have had relations with her…"

"Um, Lord Lugh, what do you mean by 'relations'?" Tarte asked, tilting her head inquisitively.

Seeing that I was having trouble answering, Dia explained it for me.

"Let's see. He's talking about all the men who have had sex with this woman."

"Eek!" Tarte squealed in shock, her cheeks blushing red. Dia, on the other hand, had lived in noble society all her life and was used to this sort of discussion.

"Hmm, so I guess she's added you to her total," grumbled Dia.

"If that were true, I wouldn't have returned so quickly. I can't give you the details, but we have a strictly business relationship. She did offer, but I thought of you, Dia, and declined," I assured Dia before embracing her. She was rigid at first but swiftly relaxed.

"…Okay, I believe you."

"Thanks. Do you believe me, too, Tarte?"

"Of course. You aren't the type to be tempted by sex, my lord."

Physical intimacy could entice me. Young bodies are naturally attracted to those kinds of advances, after all. I just didn't let it show.

"Um, Lord Lugh. You received a letter from Lord Naoise," stated Tarte.

"Hmm, how should I respond?" I wondered. "I have no lack of reasons to refuse."

"You have a lot of other invitations, too. Um, here are all the

Chapter 3

ones we got while you were gone, my lord," Tarte said before spreading a pile of envelopes on a desk.

Now that I was both a Holy Knight and a Chosen, it appeared that everyone hoped to curry favor with me.

"Not all of these are invitations to parties. This one's a mating offer," I remarked.

"You're so popular, Lugh," Dia commented.

"'Mating'? That makes you sound like a horse, my lord," Tarte interjected.

Although odd phrasing, *mating* was the correct word. The more powerful one's mana was, the more likely it was that their children would possess strong mana as well, which was what the invitation was after.

"The strength of one's magical power is a status symbol among nobles, and ethics often get thrown out the window when pursuing that coveted prize. They're asking me if I want to leave behind a child in case I die against a demon. It's just an excuse to get my mana, though," I explained.

"That's a real turnoff when you put it that way," Dia commented.

"Um, what do you think, my lord?" questioned Tarte.

"I'm with Dia. I don't even want to think about what will happen after my death," I answered.

Tarte looked disappointed.

She was probably hoping to offer her help if I wanted to have a child. Her filter had been growing looser and looser. I needed to be careful.

I ran through all of the invitations, reading Naoise's last. A full list of attendees was included in his message, each one a young person with true talent. It was a very Naoise thing to do.

"Tarte, this is my reply to Naoise. Please deliver it to him," I instructed, handing Tarte the missive.

"Yes, my lord. Ah, so you are going?" she questioned.

"Are you sure you want to go? That party is going to be full of children doing nothing but playing at knights. There are plenty of gatherings where we could make better connections," Dia interjected.

"That's harsh... There are names on this list I can't ignore. Countess Granfelt and Marquis Granvallen will both be attending."

Naoise was in danger, and I was interested in the talented folks he was assembling.

The snake demon had flashed me a suggestive smile when I left her room. She must have known we would be meeting again soon.

"Urgh, you really do just want to spend time with that big-boobed woman," Dia spat.

"...Lord Lugh, if you like sexy women like her, I-I'll do my best to satisfy you!" declared Tarte.

"I have no particular desire to see her. It's just dangerous to leave her unchecked. She's like a wolf in sheep's clothing, and no one is aware of the threat she poses," I explained.

Worst-case scenario, Naoise and all the other promising young nobles could get added to her list of victims.

Dia eyed me doubtfully. She probably would have understood if I just told her that Mina was a demon, but the agreement I'd made prevented me from doing that. I abided by any contract, no matter the other party. Thus, I needed to persuade her with a different method.

I kissed Dia. It caught her completely off guard, and her eyes went wide. Tarte covered her face with her hands, but she watched through her fingers.

"You really don't trust me? I'm telling you, Dia, I love you most of all. Let's go to the next room. I'll prove it to you with my actions," I said and picked her up in my arms. Dia did not resist.

"You can be really pushy sometimes, Lugh," she replied with a sigh.

"Do you not want to do this right now?"

"…I do. I want you to love me."

"Then let's go."

It'd been a while since I'd been with Dia. Finding time alone wasn't easy at the Tuatha Dé estate. Aside from a few exceptions like my dad's office and the torture chamber, the rooms weren't soundproof. And to make matters worse, there was a certain pair in the household who liked to strain their ears and listen attentively.

However, this was the royal castle. We could make love in peace.

"Ah, um, I'll go deliver the letter!" Tarte shrieked, red-faced. Then she dashed from our apartment.

She was trying to be tactful by giving Dia and me time alone. I would have to ensure her consideration didn't go to waste.

Chapter 4 | The Assassin Gives Warning

The next day, we went to House Gephis's villa in the royal capital.

The tea party was being held in a large courtyard. Possibly because House Gephis was known for its military prowess, the area also functioned as a training ground, and there were people at the event crossing swords and working up a sweat.

Most of the attendees were young and accomplished nobles. They craved power and attention, and they probably wouldn't have been satisfied by simply chatting over tea.

"Why didn't you two wake me up until it was almost time to go? I had to rush through my makeup," Dia complained as she straightened her dress. She looked at me reproachfully.

"I was taken by your adorable sleeping face," I answered.

"Um, you two slept together yesterday, and I thought it might be wrong for me to enter your room," said Tarte.

"W-well, I can't be angry with you two if you put it like that."

Satisfied, Dia looked at her reflection in a hand mirror. She didn't usually wear makeup, but this was a special occasion.

"You're so beautiful, Lady Dia. You look like a fairy," Tarte praised, and I was inclined to agree.

She was wearing a sky-blue dress that didn't reveal much skin, but it accentuated her beauty wonderfully. Her makeup gave her a more mature look for her age, too.

Many partygoers were unable to take their eyes off her. That made me proud as her boyfriend, but I had to stay wary of any creeps who might try to approach her.

"Thanks. I'm sure you'd look lovely in a gown, too, Tarte. You're rolling in money from your Holy Knight's salary, aren't you, Lugh? Buy Tarte a dress," Dia commanded.

"I will. I'm certain you'd look great, Tarte," I agreed.

"N-no, you can't. I'm a servant. And dresses don't look good on me," Tarte objected, flustered.

"There's no rule that says servants can't don something nice once in a while. All right, let's do it. We'll have you wear a dress at the next party. How about I have Maha prepare an extravagant gown just for you?" I suggested.

The outfit Dia was wearing had also been arranged by Maha. You didn't see dresses this nice very often, even at parties in the royal castle attended by noted noble families. Money alone wasn't enough to obtain a garment like this—you also needed proper connections and preparation.

"Um, that would really be a waste. Dresses just don't look good on me."

"You're beautiful, Tarte. I haven't seen a single servant better looking than you at any of the social functions we've been present at in the castle. And more than anything, I want to see what you'd look like in a dress," I stated.

"Yeah, drop the modesty, Tarte. You're gorgeous. Also, you have big boobs. Really, really big boobs. Super mega boobs. You would look good in something revealing," added Dia.

"Ah-ha-ha-ha, thank you very much," responded Tarte with obvious unease. Her face twitched at the repetitious use of *boobs*.

Chapter 4

Dia had a complex about her chest. I'd seen her staring wistfully at a low-cut gown when she was picking her outfit.

After a while, the three of us reached the center of the courtyard where Naoise and his followers were gathered.

"Thank you for coming, Lugh," Naoise said.

"I was interested to see what kind of party you would put on, Naoise," I replied, only saying as much to be polite. My biggest concern wasn't Naoise; it was the voluptuous, grinning woman behind him. She was currently surrounded by young knights.

The men at the party were already losing themselves over Mina's seductive charm. Even those who had been taken by Dia's beauty and stalking us from a distance now only had eyes for the demon.

The strength of her pheromones truly was something.

Mina grinned and waved, and I responded with a slight bow. Dia's grip on my arm tightened, and Tarte tugged at my sleeve.

"Do you mind if I introduce you to everyone?" asked Naoise.

"I suppose that would be fine," I answered hesitantly.

Naoise shepherded me to the highest point in the courtyard.

"Attention, everyone, I have someone I'd like you all to meet. This is Lugh Tuatha Dé, a school friend of mine, as well as a Holy Knight and slayer of demons."

Upon Naoise's words, all present turned to look at me, adoration plain in their eyes. Because they were still young, they didn't gaze upon me with greed or self-interest, as most aristocrats would. Instead, they resembled children gawking at a knight in a picture book.

Judging that to be the sort of vibe expected of me, I decided to indulge them a little.

"Yes, I'm Lugh Tuatha Dé. I've been appointed a Holy Knight, and I am currently fighting demons."

Every attendee outranked me in the social hierarchy, but I still used my casual speaking tone. The audience expected me to be a living legend. Humility was not what they wanted. My self-introduction was brief, but it still sent a wave of excitement racing through the venue.

"I called Lugh Tuatha Dé here today so he could learn of our existence. Auguide Order, assemble!"

Upon Naoise's command, the young men at the party gathered in perfect formation.

"Draw your blades!"

Each person introduced himself and drew his sword, holding it still in front of his chest. The introductions moved from one side of the group to the other, traveling like a wave.

It was a beautiful performance, and the display made it clear that the troop had undergone intense physical training. Their total lack of extraneous movement was a testament to their many hours of practice.

There was no doubt that everyone here was decently skilled with a sword and had a good teacher. Naoise had likely arranged that.

"We are the knights of the Auguide Order! We devote our swords to the peace of the kingdom!" Naoise exclaimed at the end of the demonstration. All of the young nobles looked quite proud of themselves.

...*Ah, I see. That's what's going on here.*

Auguide was a chivalrous figure from an old fairy tale. That they had chosen that name told me a lot about the collective mindset of the youths who had joined Naoise's league.

"Lugh, this is my knighthood, the Auguide Order. All

gathered here are either sons of noted families who own villas here in the royal capital or capable talents whom I found at the Royal Academy. I brought them together, gained the sponsorship of House Gephis, and earned official recognition as this country's second company of magic knights."

With the demons having returned, monsters were reappearing at a much higher rate. Typically, each region fended off the creatures on their own, but with the recent increase in numbers, that had become difficult. Many areas were asking for help from the kingdom, and the Royal Order was presently dispatched throughout the country.

However, even the resources of the Royal Order were limited, and there was no way they could aid everyone. That must have given Naoise his idea.

He'd searched for potential in aristocratic youths who had not yet inherited their house and commoners who bore no ties of obligation, and he had found a way to put them to use.

The central government had no reason to object to a new company of knights if House Gephis was funding it. What's more, the organization was the brainchild of Naoise, one of the hero's companions.

"Our group is still small. However, every knight here is strong and brimming with passion. We already have a few triumphs under our belt, and that will only continue as time goes on. One day, we will be more decorated and respected than even the official Royal Order," boasted Naoise.

So this is how he intends to change things in Alvan.

I doubted Naoise had merely been inspired by a knight from an old fairy tale like the others. It was more likely he was using the name to manipulate the sense of honor these young men felt.

No matter the era, playing to feelings of righteousness was an effective tool for controlling impressionable minds.

"So are you inviting me to join the Auguide Order, too?" I asked.

"No, I am not. But when the next demon appears, we will fight with you. That is why I wanted to introduce you to everyone today. Given that the hero can't leave the royal capital, you are the world's greatest hope, and it is our duty to support you."

The members of the Auguide Order nodded proudly.

Playing a role in defeating a demon would certainly boost the Auguide Order's reputation. If all went well, they could come to hold more influence than the Royal Order. I understood Naoise's line of thought. Because I thought of him as a friend, I chose my next words carefully.

"I don't need your help. Don't get involved in our fight against the demons. You'll get in my way."

At my statement, the courtyard went silent, and Naoise's face stiffened.

I knew this would happen, but I'd had no choice but to say as much. If I hadn't, it would have been only a matter of time before these men lost their lives. They may hate me for it, but at least they'd survive. None of them understood they were playing at being saviors. Reality wasn't some fairy tale.

Chapter 5 | The Assassin Makes a Wager

Faces that had been filled with hopeful admiration contorted in bewilderment and silent anger. The Auguide Order had not expected rejection from a Holy Knight. They'd anticipated that I'd ask them to join my side while saying how much I expected of them all. That was what I should have done if all I cared about was making sure everyone got along.

However, I couldn't patronize them. I didn't want these young people, and especially not my friend Naoise, to die.

"Ha-ha-ha, Lugh's got a rough sense of humor. I'm sure he's just trying to get us fired up," Naoise said with a smile, trying to salvage the situation.

"No, I'm serious. As someone who has actually fought demons, I know that fighters of merely adequate skill would only hold me back. When fighting a creature that powerful, I won't have any time to protect you all," I stated firmly.

I recalled the battle with the beetle demon and how Tarte had fought up close then.

Her capabilities had been enhanced by the power of My Loyal Knights, her S-Rank skill Beastification, and even the drug I'd developed. Yet despite all of those boosts, it took everything she had to buy me the time I'd needed.

S-Rank skills granted legendary power and were normally

only possessed by one in one hundred million people. Tarte possessed *two* of those abilities, and she still couldn't match a demon's raw might. Such was the sort of foe we faced.

A demon would undoubtedly lay waste to common warriors without so much as breaking a sweat.

"If that's true, then what about Dia and Tarte? You took them along. According to the report you submitted, they both contributed greatly to your victory. I know how talented those two are, but I am confident that I possess strength equal, no, superior to them. And the Auguide Order is composed entirely of brave men who have earned my personal approval," argued Naoise.

If we were going by grades from our time at the Royal Academy, Naoise was indeed ranked higher than Dia and Tarte. However, they hadn't displayed their full power at school, and they'd become much stronger since its temporary closure.

"Allow me to ask one question, then. Is there anyone here who can use Demonkiller?" I inquired.

Demonkiller was a spell that Dia and I had created, although as far as the public knew, it had been bequeathed to me by the goddess. Recently, information on how to use Demonkiller had been made public.

There was no way the Auguide Order, eager for glory as they were, hadn't tried casting that magic.

Eyes cast down, Naoise admitted, "...There is no one in our order who can use it."

"Then tell me, how are you going to slay a demon? If you read my report, then surely you know that Tarte kept the demon in place, Dia cast Demonkiller, and I finished it off. In short, if you can't use Demonkiller, then I can't accept your assistance."

"Well, but... What if we help restrain the demons? From the

next mission on, we will perform Tarte's role. That has to be more efficient than her doing so alone," Naoise countered.

While shaking my head, I answered, "I told you earlier. A fight against a demon could go awry at any moment. I won't be able to protect you."

"Are you suggesting that Tarte is more capable than all of my knights and me combined?"

"I am."

Unsurprisingly, that answer seemed to injure Naoise's pride. He threw down his glove at Tarte's feet.

"...If you won't rescind that statement, then I have to request a duel. My pride demands satisfaction," Naoise declared.

"Huh? U-um, you want to fight me?" questioned a flustered Tarte.

"If I beat her in a duel, then surely that will prove what you just said to be wrong. My victory means we will join you in the fight against demons."

Utterly at a loss, Tarte looked to me.

"We have no reason to accept," I responded.

"Should I lose, you may ask me for anything, so long as it is something House Gephis can grant," answered Naoise.

The power of a duke's house, huh?

A duke's house could do just about anything, but I still didn't find the stakes very tempting. That said, I didn't see any other way to get control of this situation.

"Tarte, please accept the duel. And don't hold back."

"Y-yes, my lord. I will do my best. But is it really okay for me to go all out?"

If Tarte was to fight at full strength, it would mean using Beastification. She was worried that doing so might lead to Naoise being seriously injured. Her inquiry was born of concern, yet to Naoise, it seemed a biting insult.

"...Tarte. It seems as if you are severely underestimating my ability. It hurts to know that you think so little of me."

"Oh, um, sorry. I didn't mean it that way..."

"It's fine. Say no more. I will prove my strength in our duel."

Naoise left it at that and stepped into a ring in the courtyard. One of his knights handed him a wooden sword. Tarte appeared panicked and on the verge of tears, but after I nodded to her, she joined him.

Naoise looked at her blankly.

"My apologies. I was inconsiderate. You surely can't fight in those clothes. Please change before we begin," he requested.

Naoise was in ceremonial attire, but because House Gephis prided themselves on their military prowess, the garments were made with combat in mind. Tarte, however, was wearing her maid outfit.

"No, I am fine. My lord made these clothes for me. They may not look like much, but they're stronger than most armor," Tarte responded.

That applied to all of Tarte's uniforms. She was often at my side in servant attire, and I wanted to ensure she was always combat-ready. I had made the garments using materials from monsters, then strengthened the clothing with magic to ensure it provided Tarte with both mobility and defensive strength.

The only issue was the skirt. It was considered vulgar in Alvan for women to wear pants in public. Thus, I'd had no choice but to try making a skirt suitable for combat.

Tarte's blade-proof knee-high socks meant there was no need to worry about injuries to her legs, but any intense movement would cause her hem to flutter up.

I didn't want anyone catching sight of Tarte's underwear, so I decided to protect her by controlling the wind without anyone noticing.

"I never would have thought that uniform offered any protection. That means I don't have to restrain myself," Naoise said with a sigh of relief. Even after feeling insulted, he still displayed concern for Tarte. Knowing what Naoise was like, that wasn't too surprising.

He had been taken with Tarte since the beginning. What interested me, however, was that his feelings didn't seem to be romantic. Were I to describe it, I would say it more closely resembled a son longing for a mother. Perhaps Tarte resembled Naoise's.

"Tarte, go all out and finish him in one blow," I instructed.

"Yes, my lord," she responded.

"Just how far do you plan to take this ridicule, Lugh?" Naoise asked, visibly offended.

"You'll see whether or not this is ridicule after the duel."

Tarte picked up a wooden lance. She took a deep breath and focused herself. "U-um, Lord Naoise. The moment the duel begins, I am going to close the distance between us in one step and swing at your waist horizontally from just inside my spear's range. Please block it... I don't want to kill you."

Rage crossed Naoise's face. Tarte's last statement had really pushed him over the edge. "...Let's cut the talking. I will have my honor." The young man readied his sword. It was an orthodox stance that gave him a perfect guard.

The two combatants turned to face each other.

One of Naoise's knights was serving as the judge. He raised a flag. The duel would commence when he lowered it.

Tarte looked at me, and I nodded in approval. At that, her fox ears and tail appeared. Someone in the crowd of onlookers remarked how cute she was. That a person was willing to express that feeling in this situation said a lot about how perfectly the fox ears and tail complemented Tarte's looks.

Despite facing off against Naoise, Tarte appeared totally unbothered. Her normally timid eyes had taken on the sadistic glint of a hunter. The side effects of Beastification were pushing her into an excited state.

My maid was normally hesitant and unable to exert her full strength, but Beastification allowed her to show no mercy. I was confident she would strike quick and hard.

"Begin!"

The flag came down.

Immediately, Tarte vanished, followed by a delayed sound.

She charged at Naoise too swiftly to follow without Tuatha Dé eyes, her movements extremely precise. Just as she had declared, Tarte brought her weapon to bear with a horizontal slash at Naoise's waist, and the young noble barely managed to meet it. That he did was a testament to his skill, of course, but he never would've been able to had Tarte not informed him of her plan of attack.

The wooden sword and wooden spear collided and splintered upon impact, but Tarte pushed through and completed her stroke. Before the wooden spear snapped completely, it sent the wooden sword flying, and Naoise along with it.

He went tumbling out of the ring and bounced on the ground several times before colliding with a storehouse erected at the edge of the courtyard.

"I win. My lord, I ended it in one hit, just like you told me to!" Tarte exclaimed with a cheerful and innocent voice, wagging her fluffy fox tail.

The knights gaped in disbelief that quickly shifted to fear.

Naoise was the strongest member of their order, and the young man had just been handily trounced not by the Holy Knight, but by his servant.

Naoise walked back toward us while gripping his side and dragging his feet. A few of his ribs were broken.

"Naoise, this is Tarte's current level of strength, and even she was overwhelmed by the demon. It took all she had to keep it still for less than a minute, and if the fight had gone on any longer, she would have died. Do you understand now?" I said.

Despair showed on the knights' faces. They had known that demons were strong, but they had underestimated the depths of that might. This demonstration had been a wake-up call. There was no way any of them believed winning glory by defeating a demon was still achievable.

With a hollow look in his eyes, Naoise returned to the ring and grabbed Tarte's hand. "Tell me! Tell me how you obtained that strength! I need…to grow stronger…"

That was all he managed before collapsing.

"Someone call a healer!"

"Send for a doctor, quickly!"

"Is there a stretcher anywhere?!"

A few members of the Auguide Order went off in search of a mage who knew healing magic.

Tarte looked frightened, even though Beastification was still active. That was how dreadful Naoise's expression had been. Her fox ears and tail disappeared, and she hastened to my side.

"Um, was what we did okay, my lord?" she asked.

"Yes, it's best they understand the magnitude of the situation. Anything less might leave Naoise and his group willing to seek out a demon on their own," I answered.

It was a shocking method, but there'd been no other option. If Naoise had lost in a duel to me, he and his fellows would have written it off as due to my being a Holy Knight, and it wouldn't have deterred them at all. Failing against Tarte, however, left no room for argument.

Hopefully they understand their place now.

"I feel a little bad for him."

"You're a nice person, Tarte."

I patted her head, and while she appeared a little embarrassed, she accepted the gesture gladly.

It was time for us to go. I had a feeling we were no longer welcome here. We could follow up with Naoise later, but there was one final piece of business I had to settle.

Mina was standing alone, looking bored. The crowd of knights that had been around her had vanished when Naoise had fainted.

"What are you doing here?" I demanded.

"Hmm, I thought it would be fun. I find young people and their passion so much more stimulating than the greasy old men who attend most parties… And that boy's last expression before he passed out was delicious. He looked so full of despair he could cry, but he was still bursting with ambition and a real thirst for strength. It set my heart racing," Mina responded wickedly.

"That's my friend you're talking about. If you lay a hand on him, you'd better be prepared for the consequences," I cautioned.

"What are you getting upset for? I'm not breaking our agreement. And I'm not going to do anything bad to him. Not really."

"You're not the only one who can skirt around violating our contract, you know."

"Oh? Hmm-hmm, now that's exciting."

I'll need to use Illig Balor's information network to keep an eye on Naoise for a while. I can't give this snake demon a chance to go after him.

I also decided I would take one more defensive precaution. Grabbing one of the knights who had been running around in a panic, I told him, "After Naoise wakes up, tell him that he and the entire Auguide Order must stay away from Countess Granfelt as his favor to me for losing the duel."

"Hey, that's not fair," Mina protested.

"You're the one who started this. This is beyond the scope of our agreement. You have no right to interfere with any promises made between Naoise and me."

"Aww, I guess you're right. That's too bad. I was going to have some real fun with him. I'll back off...this time."

And with that, I achieved the goal of protecting Naoise and his knights from Mina's schemes. I had no doubt that Naoise would uphold his promise to obey my request.

"Tarte, Dia, let's go," I stated.

Tarte bobbed her head. "Yes, my lord."

"Let's stop somewhere on the way back. I didn't get to eat anything," said Dia.

The three of us left the Gephis villa behind.

Where will Naoise and his knights go from here? I wondered.

I'd managed to dissuade them from joining me in the fight against demons. There was no guarantee they wouldn't do anything else reckless, however.

Still, this was as much help as I could provide them. I only prayed that my friend wouldn't stray from the path.

Chapter 6 | The Assassin Gives His Consent

After Naoise's party, we returned to the castle apartment that was on loan.

The thirst for power Naoise had displayed before collapsing weighed heavy on my mind. If that desire ever outgrew his pride, it would be the perfect opportunity for Mina to pounce.

She was a demon, after all. It was conceivable she had a way of granting strength to a human.

I used an underground communications network to contact Maha and had her prepare surveillance. Afterward, Tarte, Dia, and I headed to our respective rooms to bathe and change. Then we reconvened in the common room. We exchanged idle chatter for a bit.

"This place is so convenient. I wish we could live here forever. They provide us with any goods or services we ask for," Dia remarked.

"As a servant, I haven't known what to do with myself. I feel like I have no reason for being here...," Tarte confessed.

"It's definitely comfortable, but I feel more at ease in Tuatha Dé, and I prefer Tarte's food," I responded.

"I'm happy to hear you say that, my lord."

Dia's eyes narrowed slightly. "I knew that you preferred the domestic type, Lugh. I need to learn how to cook. My mom always said the way to a man's heart is through his stomach."

"*Ahem.* Anyway, let's talk about tomorrow." In addition to Naoise's event, there had been one other invitation among the heap I'd received that I couldn't refuse. "I am meeting with Duke Romalung tomorrow… He sent me an invitation with the king's signature on it. That means there's no avoiding this. He wants to meet with us directly."

House Romalung was one of the four major dukedoms, like Naoise's family. It also had a deep connection to the secret operations of the Tuatha Dé clan.

We fought only for the well-being of the nation. As such, we operated strictly on orders from the royal family.

However, our orders didn't always come from the royal family directly. House Romalung vetted missions first to decide if they were truly in the country's best interest, then passed them on to House Tuatha Dé. They also handled the aftermath of our assassinations.

In other words, they were the boss of the Tuatha Dé clan.

"Hmm, I wonder if it would be okay for me to go, too," wondered Dia aloud.

"I don't think so. They said in the letter I can take one attendant and no one else," I explained.

"What do you think would happen if you disobeyed and I came along anyway?"

"The king's seal is on this missive. Failure to comply could mean death."

"Yikes. Never mind, then. Watch over Lugh for me, Tarte."

"Yes, Lady Dia! I will protect Lord Lugh even if it costs me my life!" Tarte exclaimed with great enthusiasm.

"I appreciate the eagerness, but make sure you take care of yourself, too. You're important to me, Tarte, and I'd be sad if you got hurt," I said.

Tarte's cheeks flushed red, and she put her hands to her face. "Wha?! Me, important..."

"Lugh, you have a real habit of blurting out overly serious things," Dia stated.

"I'm only making an effort to tell people how much I care about them. Especially you, Tarte, and Maha."

We were a team. I wanted as few secrets between us as possible. Admittedly, I had to hide a lot from them. Perhaps that's where my desire to be more open came from.

Dia folded her arms. "Hmph. How do you think it feels when you tell us things like that but then continually ignore us? We need to step up our efforts. Lugh's been thinking of his precious boob lady nonstop lately. It seems like we aren't enough for him. We need your sex appeal, Tarte."

"S-sex appeal?" repeated Tarte.

"Yeah, I have no problem with you. I'd much rather you satisfy Lugh than have some old hag hog all the attention."

I let out an exasperated sigh. "...How many times do I need to tell you? I don't see Countess Granfelt that way."

"I know. I believe you, Lugh. You think of her as an enemy. I was just teasing. I'm gonna go back to my room to finish the magic I started on earlier today," Dia replied. "Also, I want to concentrate today, so I'm going to put earplugs in. When I get really focused on my research, I tend to become oblivious to the world. So good luck," she added conspicuously before leaving.

I looked at Tarte, and her cheeks reddened even further. She then opened her mouth to speak, looking as if it was taking a great amount of effort to get the words out. "Um, my lord, do you remember our discussion about how I'd be able to better serve you if I enticed assassination targets with my body?" she asked timidly.

"I remember. I put a stop to that," I responded.

Seduction was definitely a powerful tool for covert killing, and it had been employed since ancient times. Tarte was beautiful, she had a very attractive body, and her gentle demeanor was alluring in its own right.

However, Tarte's personality wasn't cut out for that kind of work. More importantly, I didn't want Tarte involved in that sort of thing.

"I remember what you told me after I said I wished to learn how to use my body not as an assassin, but to service you as a maid. 'Let's save that for another day. I don't feel like sleeping with a girl who started shaking just because a man threw her down on the bed.'"

"I did say that."

Tarte somehow remembered what I'd said word for word.

"Could that day be today?"

"Where is this suddenly coming from?"

"It's not sudden! I've always wanted you to love me, but I've been a little scared. I've been working really hard to get over my fear so that the day you mentioned would come. I've been holding back for a while. But then you did it with Dia, and you've been looking at that sexy woman nonstop… I just can't wait any longer."

Tarte had appeared fine to me, but she must have been bothered by the snake demon and my night with Dia. Still, any concerns about the former were baseless.

Chapter 6

"Tarte, let's just calm down for now," I stated. She made a face like the world was ending. It seemed I'd said the wrong thing. "It's not that I wouldn't like to sleep with you, but you're probably still feeling the effects of Beastification. If you make a decision like that when you don't have a clear head, you'll regret it."

"I'm completely fine! I've been thinking about this for a very, very long time! And the only reason I'm able to say any of this right now is because I feel overcome by desire!"

Arousal must have been affecting Tarte's speech. Her proclamation startled me.

"You were really scared last time. Are you sure you're okay with this?"

"I've been studying! And I want you so badly that I'm not scared at all!"

"Studying, huh? So that's why you were pressing your ear to the door and listening to me and Dia yesterday."

"HUH?!? N-no way, you noticed that?"

"Of course I noticed. I'm an assassin."

"Ah, uh, well, I'm sorry... I just couldn't help myself."

"I'll let it go this time. But don't do it again. If you want to listen to us that badly, get permission from Dia first."

"I'll never do it again!" Tarte responded immediately.

I pulled her toward me forcefully, hugged her, and ran a hand across her skin.

"It seems like you really are okay."

Last time, she was shaking, and her body went stiff when I touched her, yet she remained relaxed now. Tarte accepted my embrace gently, even squeezing me back.

"I'm not scared anymore, my lord. So please."

"I can see that. Shall we go to my room?"

"Yes… Please allow me to pleasure you."

It was very like Tarte to put my wants before asking me to be gentle with her. She always thought of me first. She was a really good girl. I wanted to take good care of her and treat her affectionately.

This was her first time, so I needed to ensure she had the best possible experience.

Chapter 7: The Assassin Has a Clandestine Meeting

I woke up at my usual time. When I looked to the side, I saw a naked Tarte with her arms wrapped around me. She was smiling happily and drooling.

Totally at peace. She looked adorable.

"Lord Luuugh... You're all mine, Lord Luuuugh," she muttered, hugging me with impressive strength.

Tarte rubbed her cheeks against me, softly biting at me in her sleep, smiling all the while. It was as if she was insisting that I belonged to her. Being able to do that while unconscious was quite a skill.

Although she tried to hide it, Tarte could be quite possessive. Evidently, sleeping with her had only strengthened that character trait.

"Hmm, I don't really like going back to sleep once I'm awake," I muttered to myself.

It looked like it would be really difficult to get out of bed without waking her up. We still had time before we had to go meet Duke Romalung, so I decided to enjoy Tarte's sleeping face a while longer.

◇

Slowly, Tarte's sleepy eyes stirred and opened.

"Good morning, my lord… Huh? It's already this late?! I'm so sorry! I'll get to work on breakfast!"

Panicked, she jumped out of bed and fell to the ground. She was naked, so she ended up giving me quite a view.

"Relax. I would have woken you had I needed to. You worked hard late into the night, so I wanted to let you rest."

"Oooh, oooooh…"

Tarte started making weird noises, and her face turned the color of a tomato. She was overheating. Undoubtedly, she was recalling what had happened. She'd really given her best effort.

"I'm sorry, I forgot myself," she apologized.

"It's fine. I'm relieved to know it felt good for you. It's also more fun for me to see you so disheveled," I responded.

"You gave me so much last night! I'll study hard so I can pleasure you more next time!"

"If you want to learn, then I'll teach you myself… I'm afraid of what might happen if I leave you to figure it out on your own."

Tarte had tried hard to satisfy me despite it being her first time, but her incomplete knowledge had led her to make some mistakes. It was a bit of a difficult experience in that sense.

Obviously my mother was responsible for that.

I was confident she had filled Tarte's head with all kinds of nonsense. I could picture Tarte blushing and nodding furiously to everything that came from that woman's mouth.

"I'll do my best!"

"Put on some clothes first. It's torture watching your alluring body like this."

"Aaah! I-I'm so sorry!" Tarte screamed, only now realizing

she was naked. She covered her chest with both hands and sat down on the ground.

I turned my back to her, and before long, I heard Tarte getting dressed.

"Um, my lord, by 'torture,' do you mean it was putting you in…in that kind of mood?"

"I guess, yeah."

"Then how about I give you some morning service? Mothe…I mean, I read in a book that men love that kind of thing."

Just where did she hear something like that? Also, is my mother having Tarte refer to her as her mother-in-law? She's taken quite a liking to her.

"Maybe next time. For now, I'm hungry. Please start on breakfast," I requested.

"Yes, my lord. I'll make you something especially delicious this morning," Tarte declared, and she left the room.

Dia and I gathered at the table when Tarte had finished her cooking. We were having fluffy omelets filled with bacon and mushrooms, along with cheese toast and vegetable soup.

"Tarte, your omelets are amazing today," I commended her.

"I had good ingredients," she explained.

"I really like today's breakfast, too. So much that I hope you make it again. This is the best meal we've had in a while. Guess that's the power of love," Dia remarked.

"Huh? Love? What do you…?" Tarte squeaked, blushing.

"Dia, I've been curious. Why did you spur on Tarte like that?" I questioned.

It was normal, even expected, for nobles to have multiple wives, but that was something many women found difficult to accept, and they went along with it because they had no choice.

"I had a number of reasons." Dia brought a piece of omelet to her mouth, then continued speaking after swallowing. "The first was because I think of Tarte as a friend. I felt bad for her."

"What's the second?" I pressed.

"My duty as a noble. It will be my job as your wife to help ensure your bloodline continues. The last reason was for your sake. No matter what happens, Tarte will protect you until the end. That's the kind of girl she is. I thought you making love to her would prevent those feelings from changing."

"My feelings for Lord Lugh will never falter," Tarte protested.

"Probably. But living with unrequited love over an extended period of time is hard. You may have been fine for a while, but who knows how you'd have felt in the future? That's why I wanted you to sleep with her, Lugh—to ensure that she'll protect you."

Dia finished eating and placed her utensils down.

"This is probably an unfair question at this point, but I'm going to ask anyway… If you didn't have those three reasons, would you have been against Tarte and me having sex?" I inquired.

"Of course. I want to be your only love," Dia answered immediately.

I didn't know what to say.

"But I do have those reasons. Tarte is a friend and I want her to be happy, and multiple women is best for producing an heir. I want you guarded by someone willing to lay down their own life. When I consider all of that, it outweighs my desire to keep you to myself. Ah, Tarte, is there any dessert?"

"Oh yes. Today's is orange jelly," the maid responded.

"Nice. Give me a large helping, please," requested Dia.

"I'll fetch it right away."

Tarte disappeared into the kitchen.

Dia sighed. "Lugh, don't make me say those kinds of things. Putting those feelings into words is embarrassing."

"Thanks," I replied.

"You're welcome. Good luck this afternoon. It looks like I can't go with you, so I'll pray for your safety as I work on developing spells today."

"Please do. Let's take a different route on the way back home to Tuatha Dé. There's a path that passes through a famous tourist spot. It would be perfect for a date."

"That sounds great. I look forward to it."

Dia and I smiled at each other.

She'd been so considerate. I needed to find a way to repay her.

When afternoon came, Tarte and I left the apartment. I was wearing ceremonial clothes specially made for the Holy Knight, and Tarte was in servant attire.

My outfit had been fashioned from exquisite materials, but it was not made for combat. It wouldn't do much to defend me, there was nowhere to hide any assassination tools, and most importantly, it was difficult to move in because the attire prioritized appearance over all else.

I wanted to avoid wearing these garments, but if there was even the slightest chance of my encountering a member of the royal family, I had no other choice.

Undoubtedly, I would have to don these clothes more in the

future, so I thought it wise to create an identical set that was more suited to battle.

"Um, have you ever met Duke Romalung, my lord?" asked Tarte.

"Not directly, no. But I know what kind of person he is. He's a brilliant man, and he is unbelievably loyal," I answered.

The jobs sent to the Tuatha Dé clan told me what kind of man he was. He was highly calculating, very cautious, and extremely faithful to his country.

All of our previous assassination jobs had been for the benefit of Alvan. Some had been helpful to Duke Romalung as well. However, the duke never sent us requests that solely advanced his agenda. Despite being in a position he could abuse, he only acted on the kingdom's behalf.

That didn't mean he was a totally innocent aristocrat who gained absolutely nothing from this arrangement. If a plan that aided the country also happened to suit him, he would enact it. On the other hand, he was not hesitant when it came to jobs that were to his disadvantage.

His sole consideration was Alvan. Duke Romalung possessed the talent to realize the greatest possible benefit for the country, and above all, he was fiercely loyal to the kingdom.

"He's an amazing person," said Tarte.

"Yeah, that's what makes him scary," I replied.

This was a man who did not fear executing a plan that worked to his detriment. In other words, he would cast aside the Tuatha Dé clan in an instant if we were ever judged to be harmful to the kingdom.

"We've arrived. I can't believe we're still inside the palace," remarked Tarte.

Nodding, I said, "I've heard about this place, but I never thought I'd get to see it for myself."

We had reached a section of the royal castle called the Alvan Garden, named after the nation. It was said to be a paradise. The kingdom proclaimed it to be the most beautiful place in the world.

A diverse variety of flowers were collected here, all arranged in the most pleasing manner, and jewels and pieces of art were placed liberally throughout.

It truly was the most beautiful and extravagant location in the world. Consequently, entry was extremely restricted... The duke had likely chosen this location as our meeting spot so that nothing would be overheard.

Tarte's eyes went wide as saucers as she beheld the many splendors of the garden. Truthfully, I had a similar reaction. I wished I could have brought Dia along.

"Sir Lugh, please come this way," called a servant. She showed us through the verdant conservatory. After a moment, I realized that the young woman wasn't merely an attendant, but the daughter of a high-ranking noble family.

A certain status was required to enter this place, even if you were waiting on another. An exception was made for Tarte because she served a Holy Knight.

The young woman brought us to a gazebo in the middle of the garden—the perfect spot to talk, drink tea, and partake of the view. What's more, there were two people already there.

"Princess Farina, Duke Romalung, the Holy Knight and his attendant have arrived," the servant announced.

Tarte and I stepped forward, and she positioned herself behind me.

I knew who the pair were. The first was a girl in her mid-teens with wondrous pink hair, a trait only the royal lineage possessed. The other was a man in his mid-thirties with hair so golden that it looked like real gold had melted on top of his head.

They were both so beautiful it made them look inhuman. The royal family and House Romalung practically radiated that sort of presence.

"It is an honor to meet you both. I am Lugh Tuatha Dé, son of Baron Tuatha Dé and head of the Tuatha Dé clan," I said, going to one knee and bowing my head.

I wasn't yet the head of the family, but the assassin operation had already passed to me.

"Please lift your face," requested Princess Farina.

I did as bade.

"Wow, you're really handsome. I never noticed when I saw you from a distance at parties."

"This is no time for flirting. Well met, Lugh Tuatha Dé. I have heard about you from Cian. He has called you his family's greatest achievement... I'm having a hard time deciding if your being made a Holy Knight is cause for cheer or sorrow," Duke Romalung remarked.

"I want to destroy the demons as quickly as possible so I can accomplish my duty as a Tuatha Dé," I answered.

"That is pleasing to know. Please sit. We had our best tea leaves prepared for this occasion."

I took a chair, and the servant poured me some tea. I recognized the aroma.

"How do you like it?" the princess questioned. "I love the scent. It's so relaxing."

"Me too. I feel as though I am able to get through so much

more work while drinking this tea. Hmm? Is something the matter? Do you not enjoy its smell?" said the duke.

"No, I like it fine. Natural You just started selling this, I believe, right?" I responded.

I had created this tea leaf to help me be more productive at work, and I'd tailored the recipe to suit my tastes. Obviously, I didn't hate it.

"You know about Natural You, Sir Lugh? I'm a big fan. Their cosmetics, sweets, and tea are all the best on the market. Check this out! I have a platinum member card," boasted Princess Farina.

Platinum membership was a service my company offered. In exchange for a high membership fee, customers received regular shipments of items one step up in quality compared to what could be found in Natural You's retail shops.

Natural You was an extremely popular store, and goods flew off the shelves. Despite the expense, platinum membership was popular because it guaranteed people the items they wanted. The company was practically drowning in applications.

I knew that Princess Farina was a member. The same went for Duke Romalung's wife and daughter as well.

Was it really a coincidence that they were presenting me, Natural You representative Illig Balor, with this tea?

"My mom is a member; she introduced Natural You to me," I explained.

"I think we would get along quite well. Ah, that reminds me, Natural You will soon be holding a new product launch here in the capital. I had to make a bit of a fuss for them to do so, but it worked. It sounds like Illig Balor won't be able to make it, but the proxy representative, a girl named Maha, will be attending. I was surprised to learn that a girl about my age manages Natural You. I wonder what kind of person she is. I'm looking forward to finding out," said the pink-haired princess, looking at me while wearing a smile as sweet as a flower.

I had actually fought against the new product launch. Natural You couldn't keep up with the overwhelming demand, and I didn't like the idea of devoting resources to an event designed to expand our consumer base. Despite my objections, pressure from above had forced the issue.

"Princess Farina, let's move on to why we called Lugh here. He looks like he's had enough of this topic," the duke stated.

Maintaining her grin all the while, Princess Farina explained, "Sorry, Uncle. Meeting Sir Lugh was distracting. On to the main topic. Ahem. We have a request for you not as a Holy Knight, but as a noble assassin. Please kill my older brother. He's been bewitched by Countess Granfelt and made into her puppet. As he is now, he's a lost cause who will only bring harm to the kingdom. I don't think fixing him is going to be possible, so I'd like you to dispose of him."

The young woman was requesting that I slay her sibling, yet she spoke of it as though we were still discussing tea.

Chapter 8 | The Assassin Receives a Job

"You're ordering me to kill a member of the royal family?" I asked.

The punishment for such a thing was great. Merely accepting this job could get my whole family put to death.

"Yes. It's for the greater good," answered Duke Romalung.

"You said the reason is because he has been bewitched by Countess Granfelt, but isn't it overly hasty to kill him for that?"

"No, it is more than enough reason for his elimination. There would have been no problem had he simply wanted to support his lover and shower her in gifts, but he's gone so far as to side with the noble faction. At this rate, the balance between the two political sides will crumble," the duke clarified.

"That can't be ignored. So which prince do you wish removed?" I questioned.

There were five people who could officially be referred to as princes. If you included illegitimate children, there were twelve. The severity of this issue was proportionate to who it was.

"The second prince, Ricla," clarified the princess.

Ricla was a very important person. He and his older brother were both being considered for the throne.

Originally, it looked like the next king would be the eldest son, as his achievements stood head and shoulders above his siblings'. However, the second prince had also performed spectacularly in recent years and had emerged as a rival candidate.

"We had initially planned to make Prince Ricla the next king. He was meek and simple, which made him easy to manipulate. Unfortunately, that is the exact reason Countess Granfelt set her eyes on him... It's strange. Although undeniably shy, Ricla was never an idiot. I cannot believe he would betray his country for love. I can think of a number of things that could explain his behavior—brainwashing or drugs, perhaps—but all I can know for certain is that he cannot be saved now," Duke Romalung said.

Initially, I'd thought the decision to kill Ricla was hasty, but I supposed that was just how grave the situation was. I agreed with them that eliminating him as quickly as possible was the right move.

I could not allow a prince to be the puppet of a demon. This task was worthy of a Tuatha Dé.

"Is the nature of this job why Princess Farina gave it to me directly?" I inquired.

"Yes. If Uncle were the only one here, you probably would have suspected he was trying to overthrow the royal family," replied the princess.

"That's fair. There's one big thing that is bothering me, however. Might I ask a question?"

"Go ahead."

Pressing the issue was a bit arrogant of me, but with the stakes so high, I couldn't take any chances.

"You decided that the royal family had to give the order directly. Why would you then use a body double for Princess Farina? It only leaves me feeling suspicious."

Chapter 8

Princess Farina's expression stiffened, and then a smile slowly emerged on her face.

It was different from the grin she had been wearing previously. Her expression had been sweet, but something about it felt fake. This one, however, seemed natural.

"...What makes you think that I am an impostor?" she asked.

"Your hair proves it. Women of the royal family have pink hair," I answered.

"But my hair *is* pink!"

"Indeed. It matches Princess Farina's exactly. However, while the scent is faint, I smell hair dye. It seems like you're masking it with perfume, but I can still tell that you colored your hair. The real princess would have no need to do something like that."

No one but me could have recognized this. Assassins sharpened their senses and always observed their surroundings so as not to overlook even the most trivial of things.

Because the request to kill Prince Ricla was coming from a pretender, I needed to consider the possibility that this was a trap.

"Ah-ha-ha-ha, you found me out. Even the king himself didn't see through my disguise. You really are the Tuatha Dé clan's greatest masterpiece, Lugh Tuatha Dé! I really like him, Father."

"Did you need to give up the game so quickly, Nevan?" chided Duke Romalung.

"It's okay. He's already figured it out."

The girl was actually Nevan, Duke Romalung's only daughter and my upperclassman at the academy.

"Duke Romalung, what is the meaning of this?" I questioned.

"My apologies. I meant this as a small test of sorts. Cian is truly fervent in his praise of you. I harbor no delusions of stealing the royal family's name or tricking you. I would not be surprised if you doubted my words, so allow me to prove it to you."

No sooner did he finish speaking than the servant behind us stepped forward. She took off a wig and wiped her face with a wet towel to remove her heavy makeup. She had pink hair, and her face looked identical to Nevan's.

"Nice to meet you. I am Farina. My apologies. I was personally against this little prank."

"It educated us on Sir Lugh's true capabilities, so it worked out for the best, didn't it? You doubtlessly already know that she is Princess Farina, and I am Nevan Romalung. I was serving as her body double," said Duke Romalung's daughter.

"I am Lugh Tuatha Dé. I am pleased to make your acquaintance, Princess Farina."

I stood up and kneeled to show my fealty to the crown.

"Please stand. I saw you kneel earlier, so you have no need to do it again. I leave the rest to you, Duke Romalung," Princess Farina stated, bowing her head.

She was a humble person. With her and Nevan sporting pink hair, it was admittedly difficult to tell which was the genuine article. They very nearly appeared to be twins.

Seeing my puzzlement, Duke Romalung smiled at me. "Nevan and Farina look a lot alike, don't they? They're cousins. That is why Princess Farina calls me Uncle."

"It must be easy for you two to disguise yourselves and switch places," I remarked.

"Yes. You are the first person to ever see through the ruse. As you can see, this is a legitimate order from the royal family. Does that put you at ease?" answered the duke.

"For the most part. But I still have some doubts. Why are you working for Princess Farina, Duke Romalung? I would think you'd want to ally yourself with either the first or second prince, the ones in line for the throne."

"I do so at the behest of my friend the king. He believes Farina to be the most brilliant of his children, but she cannot become king because she's a woman. Thus, he requested that I find a way for her to wield some authority. I thought to find her a suitable husband at first, but I failed to locate a proper match. My second plan was to have Farina control Ricla. I fed the prince achievements to bolster his reputation... Regrettably, just as he was becoming an influential figure, this happened."

That explained the duke's actions. Only men could rise to positions of authority in this country. The duke had prepared a good figurehead behind which Farina could have some influence, but then he was taken from him. Now the duke had no choice but to remove the prince.

"I understand. What if I refuse?"

Duke Romalung's eyes narrowed. "I cannot guarantee your safety. You know too many things you shouldn't. Also, I'm sure you understand why we offered Natural You tea leaves and mentioned Maha by name."

"Yes, I have a good idea."

It was hard to believe they had discovered that Illig Balor and I were the same person. I didn't know for sure they had uncovered that much. Perhaps my insurance had kept them partly in the dark.

I chatted with the duke for a while and finally got the answer I was looking for.

"You and Maha are lovers, are you not? I have ascertained that there is some kind of deal between House Tuatha Dé and Natural

You. Maha has clearly taken a liking to you; she wouldn't use company resources to aid you otherwise. The young woman also went out of her way to see you at your Holy Knight ceremony. The inevitable conclusion is that you two are in a relationship."

I was relieved. It seemed like my insurance had worked.

I didn't mind if people found out there was a connection between Lugh and Maha. That actually served to further conceal my identity as Illig Balor.

Were someone to deduce that Illig and Lugh were the same person, thus proving a connection between Natural You and House Tuatha Dé, it could be disastrous. Knowing this, I had prepared evidence to make it look like Maha was supporting me because of a personal relationship. I'd hoped that once anyone came upon that, it would stop them from digging further and happening on the truth.

"Looks like I have no way out of this. I accept the job. However, I'll need support and time to make adequate preparations. I can't perform the job right away."

"I understand. You have two months. This is Prince Ricla's schedule. You decide when best to kill him," Duke Romalung said, handing me a document.

"Is that all you have to tell me?"

"Hmm. As far as was originally planned, yes. However, I have one proposal for you. Would you have any interest in marrying my niece?"

"Do you mean the princess?" I questioned, shocked.

"Yes, of course. I am losing an important piece in Prince Ricla, and I have imminent need for a new one. You would serve well. You are skilled and wise and a Holy Knight as well as a

Chosen. Surely you suit the princess just fine. I doubt becoming the next king sounds like a bad proposition to you."

"That would be wonderful, Father. I think Princess Farina and Lord Lugh are a perfect match!" exclaimed Nevan.

"If you are willing, Lord Lugh, I would ask you to consider it. I have heard so many splendid things about you," added Princess Farina.

I assumed whatever she knew about me was the result of a thorough investigation.

"I'll defer the offer for now. For both of our sakes," I answered.

I wanted to refuse outright, but doing so would have caused offense. Thus, I chose a way out that showed consideration. If I was ever outed as an assassin and Princess Farina had a connection to me, she would be ruined.

"You're so nice. I'm liking you more and more," said the princess.

Nevan looked at her cousin. "Princess Farina, if you marry Lugh, let me borrow him every now and then. I need him for House Romalung, too. Don't you agree, Father?"

"He is a very impressive man. There is no way I would object," responded the duke.

By "borrow," Nevan presumably meant for breeding purposes.

All nobles selected spouses based, to some degree, on the likelihood of producing the best possible heir. House Romalung took it to another level, however. They used all their power to pursue superior genes.

They engaged in selective breeding by taking in the best candidates they could find. I could see the results of that directly in front of me in Duke Romalung and Nevan. They both possessed inhuman beauty and incredible talent.

"Let's save this talk for another time," I suggested.

"Very well. We can revisit the topic once the assassination is finished. Let's meet again at the academy once it reopens. You'd better not ignore me… I'd be especially delighted to meet you in the dorms," Nevan said with a smile. Her natural one.

It looked like I had caught the attention of a really troublesome character.

The one saving grace was that House Romalung only desired my genetics. The worst-case scenario was sex with Nevan. Still, I planned to do my best to avoid getting roped into that.

Tarte was eying me with puffed-out cheeks, on the verge of crying. I didn't want to upset her and Dia.

Chapter 9 | The Assassin Shares a Secret

My secret meeting with Duke Romalung and Princess Farina came to an end, and Tarte and I returned to our apartment, where Dia was waiting for us.

Dia prepared tea, which was rare for her. She probably did so because Tarte was standing behind me with a dejected expression.

"Lugh looks the same as ever, but you look really tired, Tarte," Dia commented.

"I am exhausted, yet I didn't even say a single word. It was so tense in there," Tarte responded.

"You don't seem very good with that kind of thing. So did they tell you anything interesting?" Dia asked, turning her attention to me.

"Yeah, they did. We need to talk about it," I answered.

I had been given permission to discuss the job within my assassination team, so I explained the situation as we drank tea.

"Why Prince Ricla? From what you just told me, wouldn't it make more sense to assassinate Countess Granfelt? That would probably return the prince to his senses, and it would be much easier to kill a countess," Dia suggested.

"I can think of a few reasons. Until now, the second prince has been the puppet of Duke Romalung and Princess Farina. He knows how they operate. Even if he didn't have proof, Ricla would probably be able to deduce who ordered the hit... Once he did, he'd come after Princess Farina."

The second prince may have been nothing more than a figurehead, but publicly, his achievements surpassed those of Duke Romalung and Princess Farina, and he carried more authority as well. If he flexed his power and went on a rampage, things would not end well for those two.

"Yeah, I could see that," responded Dia.

"I imagine there's other reasons, too," I added. "I doubt the duke and princess believe Prince Ricla is the only person Countess Granfelt has seduced. Ricla is the biggest threat to the country, so they likely want to eliminate him first to get a handle on the situation and then observe what happens. If they kill Countess Granfelt without knowing who she has her hooks in, things could get out of control. Love is a scary thing. It leads people to do unreasonable things. I wouldn't hesitate to kill Countess Granfelt if leaving her to her own devices risked the country's imminent destruction, but that is not the case. She likes Alvan and wants to enjoy it. The duke and the princess realize that, and that's why they have decided to have the prince killed."

This had to have been Mina's plan all along. She'd used her Countess Granfelt identity to fabricate a situation where killing her was not the optimal solution, and if she ever did happen to be targeted, she could rely on her demonic strength to get out of it.

It was frustrating to accept, but Mina could destroy the kingdom whenever she pleased.

"House Romalung is amazing," Dia remarked.

"I guess. That bloodline scares me. House Romalung strives for the evolution of humanity, to eventually become 'true humans.'

Duke Romalung and Princess Farina are the product of hundreds of years of effort toward that goal," I explained.

"They want to go from humans to…humans? That doesn't make sense," Dia stated, puzzled.

"They have a different sense of values. From their point of view, the creatures we are now are incomplete. Thus, they want to gather the best parts of humanity, polish them, and become true humans. That is their line of thinking."

While House Romalung's selective breeding garnered a lot of attention, they were just as devoted to education.

Dia shuddered. "Geez, that's actually pretty creepy."

"There are a number of legends surrounding the house. First…"

I began to share some famous anecdotes about House Romalung with Dia and Tarte. One time, the family had used its military strength to start a war and wipe out an entire country, all for the purpose of obtaining superior blood.

Men in House Romalung sought one exceptional woman after another and impregnated them all. Likewise, women lay with as many first-rate men as they could. All their efforts were for the goal of expanding their number of children. House Romalung selected from that stock of offspring which would be the next generation of their family, while the remainders served them as elite vassals.

It was a very thorough process.

"That's insane," Dia said incredulously.

"I was standing behind Lord Lugh the whole time, and I was still scared of them. That was how different they felt. I was also shocked that they knew about Maha," Tarte admitted.

"I was surprised, too, but if that's all they know, then I'm not worried about it. The idea that Maha and I are lovers was actually a red herring the two of us set up. I suspected that people would be satisfied once they found that secret and wouldn't dig any deeper to find the real truth."

Maha and I being lovers was false information. I hid it well enough so that only the very best intelligence agencies would find out after giving their utmost efforts.

The harder such knowledge was to ascertain, the more reputable it would seem. That served to convince anyone who happened upon the phony documents.

It didn't take a stretch of the imagination to view my relationship with Maha that way, and the deal between Natural You and House Tuatha Dé was something I would rather have kept hidden. It was a weakness just big enough to satisfy anyone hoping to dig up something. That was why it was the perfect decoy to prevent anyone from discovering that Illig Balor and Lugh Tuatha Dé were the same person.

"You're always prepared for everything. Still, they drove us into a corner, didn't they? Even if they don't have the most important information, that doesn't change the fact that they could still hurt us by targeting Natural You or Maha. I wonder if House Romalung has some weakness we could take advantage of," Dia posited aloud.

"They do. I discovered a secret about Princess Farina and Duke Romalung during our meeting," I stated.

"Wow, great job!" praised Dia.

I doubted anyone knew I had caught on. It was something I'd noticed with my Tuatha Dé eyes.

"Princess Farina is Duke Romalung's daughter."

"Um, Lord Lugh, while it is a secret that Duke Romalung's

child serves as Princess Farina's body double, I don't think we could use that to threaten them. I am sure everyone in the royal family knows that already," said Tarte.

"Yes, Nevan is his daughter, but so is the actual Princess Farina. They're twins."

"WHAAAAAAAAAAT?!?!" cried Tarte in surprise.

"These eyes can see mana. Every person's magical power has a certain color. A parent and child's colors look similar, but the mana of twins looks identical. Duke Romalung's little brother officially married into the family of Princess Farina's mother, but there is no doubt that Princess Farina's father is Duke Romalung himself."

I had no idea what had led to it, but Duke Romalung had unquestionably sired the princess. Adultery in the royal family would be a huge scandal. Even more so because it had resulted in a child.

Duke Romalung had fathered twins with a princess. He'd left Farina with the royal family because of her pink hair and took Nevan because she did not possess the pink hair that was characteristic of the ruling family's women.

That explained why the duke was supporting Farina. He was not, however, doing so out of parental love. Whether others knew it or not, Princess Farina was a Romalung, and her triumphs would help secure the house's goals.

"They have to be crazy to commit adultery with the royal family. I feel like you're in danger as long as they have their eye on you, Lugh. Wait, why don't they just match the princess up with the hero? You're more skilled than he is, but what House Romalung wants is innate strength, right?" questioned Dia.

I guess Dia still doesn't know Epona is a girl.

House Romalung probably wouldn't have chosen Epona even if she had been a boy.

"No, what House Romalung wants to create are true humans. They see the hero and demons as monsters. They want to reach the peak of humanity, and if they stray from that, they will become nothing more than monsters themselves."

If the duke and his family desired power alone, they could try incorporating demons or monsters into their lineage. While rare, there were a few times such endeavors by other aristocratic houses had worked.

Yet House Romalung would never stoop to that level. They loved humanity; that was why they believed in, and bet on, humanity's potential.

Dia thought on that for a moment. "Oh, okay. Then you should become a hero, Lugh!"

"That's a great idea, Lady Dia. Then they would lose interest in him!" Tarte agreed.

"...If only doing so were that easy. It would solve all my problems."

The goddess could only produce one hero in the world at a time. A feat like that was beyond human capability.

"Anyway, our business in the royal capital is done. Let's return to Tuatha Dé," I stated.

"Um, what about the assassination of Prince Ricla?" inquired Tarte.

"We could do it now, but the risk would be high. Even if we leave no proof, we could be put to death the moment we're so much as suspected of killing a member of the royal family. We have two months. We should prepare as much as possible," I replied.

"That means we can finally go home," said Dia.

Tarte nodded. "I'm glad. I've been worried about the vegetable garden."

"I'd expected Tarte to be happy, but didn't you like living here, Dia?" I asked.

"It's comfortable, but it's difficult to make any progress on my research without my workshop," she answered.

The workshop in question was a terrifying place that Dia had created by completely remodeling a room in the estate. I had no idea why she needed such a place to write magic formulas, but I couldn't argue with the results. I decided to have a look at what she was working on next time she was in there.

"I see. Fair warning, we're gonna be busy when we get back home. Our fight with the last demon was a close call. We have to get stronger, and there are two major points that I think will help us do so. First, I've obtained a few appraisal sheets. We can reevaluate your fighting styles depending on what skills you have."

"Ah, you finally got some," Tarte said.

"I've always wanted to see one," added Dia.

I'd leveraged my position as a Holy Knight to get my hands on the coveted items, but it still took time to receive them. Apparently, there'd been some kind of trouble.

Learning the girls' skills would increase the number of things we could do.

"Our other avenue to improvement is turning each of our Possibility Eggs into a skill. Possibility Eggs are mirrors that reflect our hearts. I'm confident each will turn into a skill we need."

Possibility Egg transformed into a different skill that befit the owner by examining their way of life, desires, and more. It had a chance of turning into an S-Rank skill. That was why I had selected it.

Ideally, all three of us would have a new skill before the next encounter with a demon.

"But Lugh, how do we hatch them?" Dia wondered.

"I don't understand that part, either," Tarte confessed.

"Honestly, it's still a mystery to me, too, but I've been looking into it. I'm going try a variety of things to see if any work," I answered.

Maybe I'll ask Epona. It was originally her skill, so there's a chance she may know something.

I decided to meet with her before we left the capital. I also decided to ask her to look after Naoise. That thirst for power he'd displayed was troubling, as was Mina's interest in him.

I was really worried about him.

Chapter 10 | The Assassin Learns Dia's Skills

We returned to Tuatha Dé from the royal capital.

"Ahhh, it's good to be home," Dia said, stretching after we entered the estate. "Hey, Lugh, what are you laughing about?"

"Sorry. I'm not teasing you or anything. It just made me happy to see what a real Tuatha Dé you've become… I'm sure you two are tired from the long carriage ride. You should rest until lunch. We'll use the appraisal sheets this afternoon," I replied.

"I'm so nervous. I really hope I have great skills," responded Dia.

"Yes, strong skills will enable us to be of greater help to Lord Lugh," agreed Tarte.

That had been all we could talk about on the ride home.

I decided to return to my room. There was something I wanted to take care of before things got hectic.

We enjoyed a delicious lunch my mother prepared and then gathered on the training ground. I passed what appeared to be blank pieces of white paper to both Tarte and Dia. They were appraisal sheets.

"We have exactly three of them," remarked Tarte.

"We'll use them on the count of three," suggested Dia.

"I'll abstain," I said.

"Huh? Why?"

"I've used one before, so I already know my skills."

Technically, I knew my skills because the goddess had let me select them before I was reincarnated. I couldn't tell them that, however, so I just said that I'd used an appraisal sheet.

"Aww, no fair. But if you don't need one, then why did you get three?" asked Dia.

"These are normally impossible to obtain, so I thought I'd pick up an extra as a spare."

My assassination team consisted of four people: myself, Tarte, Dia, and Maha. Maha wasn't part of the field team, so there wasn't much need to know her skills. However, there was always a chance I might add another member in the future, even if I didn't have any plans to do so at the moment.

"Hmm, so you think someone new could join. If the next one is also a cute girl, I'm going to start suspecting that you're doing it on purpose," Dia remarked accusingly.

"There is a chance it could be a girl. I prioritize personality and talent when it comes to teammates. I don't make any decisions based on gender. I haven't yet, and I never will," I responded.

It had been a coincidence that my father hired Dia as my magic teacher. Similarly, happenstance led me to find Tarte after searching the entire Tuatha Dé domain for someone who possessed mana. The same went for meeting Maha at the orphanage in Milteu.

I had never once specifically searched for a girl to join my team.

"I know that, Lugh. You don't have to get so worked up. You

were so innocent when you were little. I remember how you used to always follow me around saying 'big sis, big sis!'"

That never happened. Dia was completely making that up.

"Anyway, go ahead and use your appraisal sheets. All you have to do is direct your thoughts toward them," I instructed.

"It's finally time... What will I do if I don't have any...?" Dia muttered anxiously.

"I'm not confident about this. I'm not good at anything," admitted Tarte.

"You're great at cooking, Tarte," Dia assured.

Tarte cast her eyes to the ground. "I would be really disappointed if my skills are only related to cooking..."

The girls had been brimming with excitement earlier, but now that it was time to use the sheets, they both looked anxious. Still, they seemed to have high expectations as they gripped the pieces of paper and filled them with their thoughts.

Their skills then appeared on the papers, along with an explanation for each one.

How these appraisal sheets worked was not something that could be explained with the laws of physics, magic theory, or any scientific workings. It could only be described as a miracle.

The number of people who could make the invaluable things was low, and those who could were closely guarded. There was even a rumor that they weren't human.

Seeing appraisal sheets activate with my own eyes convinced me that such a theory might hold some weight. There was no way an ordinary person could craft items so wondrous. Even if the creator was human, they must have had the help of some supernatural power.

"Phew, the paper isn't blank. That means I have skills. There are three on here," Dia said with evident relief.

"I also have three," declared Tarte.

Dia and Tarte both rushed over with their papers in hand.

"Let's take a look at them over there," I stated. I spread the sheets out on a desk placed on the training ground.

I looked at Dia's sheet first, immediately noticing that the skills she had gained from My Loyal Knights were not listed.

"I always trusted that I was good at magic, but I never knew I had this kind of skill. Also, look, I have one called Genius. Hmm-hmm, it turns out I'm truly brilliant!"

"These skills do explain some things. Your control of magic has always been otherworldly…"

Dia had one A-Rank skill, one B-Rank, and one D-Rank.

Only one in a million people possessed an A-Rank skill. That alone made Dia a special person. That she also had a B-Rank skill, something one in every ten thousand people were born with, was a statistical marvel.

Rainbow Sorcerer (A): Increases control of mana and mana output. It also grants the user the ability to change their elemental affinity at will. The change is performed by chanting a spell of the desired elemental affinity. The user will be unable to change their elemental affinity for one hour after use.

Genius (B): The user becomes a genius with superior computational skills, thinking ability, memory, and creativity.

Resistance to Aging (D): Rate of aging is slowed after the development of secondary sex characteristics.

Rainbow Sorcerer was clearly the most significant of these skills.

Chapter 10

Dia's magic precision and force were higher than normal, and she could willingly change her elemental affinity.

While I could call upon the four basic elements, I couldn't use the rare ones—light and dark. This skill would seemingly allow Dia to employ them, however.

"This is amazing. All of Lady Dia's skills seem really strong and useful!" exclaimed Tarte.

"I feel kind of like I've been wasting my talents until now, though. I had no idea I could change my elemental affinity. I've never even thought to use a spell for an elemental affinity I didn't have," Dia lamented.

Genius was an incredibly versatile skill. I had waffled between it and Limitless Growth when deciding on skills before my reincarnation.

"…Truthfully, I'm a little conflicted. I always thought it was hard work that made me a great mage. Yet now I know it was only thanks to my skills."

"That's not true. All this means is that you have natural ability. No matter how much talent you possess, it's useless if you can't figure out how to develop it. You are who you are today because of the effort you put in. I admire you for that," I reassured her.

Some people were born with ability, but they never figured out how to use it and achieved nothing. I'd seen many like that. Realizing how to put your talents to good use was challenging, and only a few managed it.

Dia raised an eyebrow at me. "You say the corniest things sometimes, Lugh."

"…I'm aware of that," I said sheepishly.

"Thanks. I'm pleased about this. I want to try changing

elemental affinities right away. I guess I should go for light or dark first. We've used the other elements plenty between the two of us."

Dia and I had created new spells by analyzing existing ones, deducing the rules, and then designing new formulas. We had divided our efforts to focus on two elements each, and we had learned nearly every spell for the four basic elemental affinities to use as material for our analysis.

However, we hadn't touched the rare affinities of light and dark. By having Dia switch to one of them and perform repeated incantations to learn new spells, we would discover new rules for creating more magic.

"I happen to have an acquaintance who can use light magic. I'll write them a letter and ask them to send me their spell formulas," I stated.

"Wow, I can't believe you actually know someone who can use light magic," said Dia.

"I only met them recently."

It had been just the other day, in fact. It was Nevan, the daughter of Duke Romalung. Her ability to use the rare light affinity had earned her the nickname Daughter of Light.

As Dia and I chatted excitedly, Tarte stared at the other girl's final skill.

"I'm jealous of your Resistance to Aging skill. You'll be pretty forever. I am sure that will make Lord Lugh happier than I ever could," she said dejectedly.

"Putting aside whether or not it'll make me happy, nobody wants to get old. That's an amazing skill… I wonder if it's passed down among women in the Viekone family. My mother undoubtedly has that skill, too."

She was over forty years old, but she could easily pass for under twenty. I had heard before that skills could become hereditary. If that was the case, it would explain my mother's unusually youthful appearance.

"I can't deny that all the women in my family look very young. I don't want this skill, though. It's definitely the reason I look like this! I'm short, and my boobs won't get any bigger! I don't know what secondary sex characteristics are, but not aging means not growing. I might've looked like Tarte if I didn't have this skill," Dia bemoaned, looking reproachfully at Tarte's chest and her own appraisal sheet.

Secondary sex characteristics continued to develop into one's late teenage years. The skill shouldn't have affected her yet, not that I was eager to volunteer that information.

"Ah-ha-ha-ha, but a big chest comes with its own problems," remarked Tarte.

"…That's what everyone with big boobs says. Anyway, that's it for me. Let's look at Tarte's!"

"Here is my appraisal sheet! I'm so happy. I also have an A-Rank skill!"

Tarte possessed an A-Rank, a C-Rank, and a D-Rank skill.

Dia and Tarte both had A-Rank skills. That couldn't have been a coincidence. Perhaps this was the result of the goddess's meddling.

Suspicious though I was, I couldn't deny feeling thankful that both girls had A-Rank skills.

Tarte's were powerful and…interesting. I couldn't help but chuckle to myself at how much her skills suited her.

Chapter 11 | The Assassin Learns Tarte's Skills

Now that I had finished looking at Dia's skills, it was Tarte's turn.

"These are so cool!" exclaimed Tarte.

"I don't know about cool, but...they're very you," Dia responded.

"Yeah, to an almost scary extent," I agreed.

The three of us read the appraisal sheet. As had been the case with Dia's, the skills from My Loyal Knights were not present.

Servant's Devotion (A): Activates upon forming a contract with a person whom the user recognizes as their master. The agreement is forged through confirmation via mucous membrane contact between master and servant. If the user's soul does not recognize the person as their master, the contract fails. The master cannot be changed. While active, all abilities of the servant and their master are strengthened. It also grants the servant the ability to sacrifice their own life to save their master in the event of their master's death.

Spear Arts (C): The bearer's physical ability is increased when they wield a spear. This also increases the force, speed, and precision of their spear attacks.

Hard Worker (D): Grants the bearer the ability and disposition to devote their full efforts to their work. Concentration and mental energy recover quickly.

"The process for activating Servant's Devotion is fine if the master and servant are opposite genders, but what would you do if both of you were the same gender...?" I wondered aloud.

"That's simple. There's nothing wrong with two people of the same gender kissing each other," responded Dia matter-of-factly.

"I suppose that's true."

Servant's Devotion, like Rainbow Sorcerer, was a skill that you likely couldn't activate unless you knew about it. Not only did it require a deep relationship with someone you recognized as a master, you then had to go out of your way to confirm that bond using a rather unusual method. It was difficult to imagine anyone would trigger it organically.

"Um, my lord, we should use this skill right away! It will make both of us stronger," Tarte stated, looking at me expectantly.

The conditions for activating Servant's Devotion were very strict, but the payoff of strengthening all abilities of both parties more than made up for it. It was undoubtedly an incredible skill.

It was significantly more potent than other A-Rank skills. Its few undesirable qualities likely kept it from being an S-Rank skill. The servant couldn't swap their master, and they had the power to sacrifice their own life to save their master's. People also tend to change over time, so there was a chance the servant could lose faith in their master.

It was also a drawback that the bearer was only empowered while Servant's Devotion was active, rather than all the time.

"Tarte, I need you to promise two things. First, I want you to make full use of the increased ability this skill offers," I began.

"Yes, my lord," she responded.

We needed to verify the rate of stamina and mana consumption as well as the extent to which we were strengthened while the skill was active, but that was still no reason not to take advantage of the boosts.

"However, you must promise me that you will not use the ability that gives up your life to save mine," I added.

Judging from the name, that was probably the main purpose of Servant's Devotion. I wanted no part of that, however.

Eyes downcast, Tarte replied, "...I'm sorry. I can't promise that. I am absolutely going to use it if the time ever comes. I will not lie to you, my lord."

"Then I won't form the contract," I decided.

I no longer thought of Tarte as a tool. I wanted no part of a skill that required a member of my family to forfeit their life.

"Lugh, I don't think that makes total sense," said Dia.

"In what way?" I asked.

"You're saying you don't want to use the skill because you don't want to sacrifice Tarte. Yet that ability can only be used if you perish. Are you planning on dying?"

"No, I'm not."

"Then don't worry about it. Servant's Devotion will make you stronger and thus harder to kill. Forgoing making yourself even more powerful and gaining greater survivability just feels silly."

Dia could have phrased it in a less confusing way, but it did make sense.

"My lord!"

I saw determination burning in Tarte's eyes. She then grabbed the back of my head and forced our lips together, drawing me into an open-mouthed kiss.

I could have avoided it, but once I saw her expression, I lost all desire to do so.

"Please become my master. And please don't die so that I

won't. Even if I didn't have this skill, if you ever disappeared…I would, too," insisted Tarte.

That's not fair, Tarte. There's no refusing if you say something like that.

"Understood. Then I'll ask this of you again. Please become my servant."

As soon as I said those words, something hot tied our two souls together. A tight bond of master and servant had just been formed.

"I feel your presence flowing within me, my lord. I know that I can use the skill now. *Servant's Devotion*," Tarte called, activating the ability.

The moment it triggered, I sensed Tarte more deeply than I ever had before. I also detected that my physical abilities, mana, mental faculties, and more were all enhanced.

Tarte touched a hand to her chest. "I've gotten stronger, and I feel so close to you, my lord. It's so peaceful. I want to stay like this forever."

"Yeah, it's a nice feeling," I agreed.

I hadn't merely acquired power. I could sense Tarte's feelings.

Actually, it went beyond that. I understood what Tarte was thinking.

Was that kiss too daring? What if Lord Lugh thinks I'm indecent? But it felt so good. I want to do it again. I'm burning up. I'll go to his room later… Wait, am I perceiving Lord Lugh's thoughts? What?! No way! Uhhhh, ah, yes, meat is good for dinner tonight. Understood. Huuuuuuuhhhh?!

It seemed like we could read the other's mind while the skill was active. I decided to experiment with it a bit.

Tarte, if you can hear me, raise your right hand.

Chapter 11

Tarte, if you can hear me, kiss me one more time.

I ran two different ideas through my brain at the same time. One was a surface-level notion, while the other was more repressed.

Tarte raised her right hand. However, she did not kiss me.

Evidently, the skill didn't share those thoughts kept more deeply within the mind.

As a countermeasure, assassins could willingly sort mental concepts and memories between the surface or the depths of their brains. If someone were to use truth serum on me, the only information they would glean would be from the upper levels of my brain, leaving all intelligence from the lower portions untouched. This was an ability one had to train to acquire.

It enabled me to keep Tarte from learning things I didn't wish her to.

Tarte's face had grown so red that it looked like steam could start blowing from her ears.

Ohhhh, I'm so embarrassed. I can't think anything weird—especially not anything indecent. Wait, can he hear me telling myself not to think indecent things?! That's embarrassing, too. I need to stop thinking entirely to be safe... Lord Lugh's pecs are so...NO, STOP! Trying to keep my mind quiet is making my head hurrrrrt...

This power seemed dangerous for Tarte. I found it funny, though.

Being able to read each other's minds may have seemed like a drawback at first, but it could serve us very well if we used it for telepathic communication. The ability to relay concepts in real time without speaking would undoubtedly be a huge advantage.

"Lugh, why are you just standing there grinning?" Dia questioned.

"Tarte's been making me laugh," I explained. "Did you feel any fatigue when you activated the skill, Tarte?"

"Huh? N-no, not at all," she replied.

"I see. Let's perform a few tests, then."

Now that Tarte had activated the skill, I decided we might as well try some things out.

The first thing I confirmed was the area of effect. I moved away from Tarte until our connection was finally severed at roughly two hundred meters. When I came toward her again, we did not automatically reconnect.

Tarte attempted to activate her skill again but found that she couldn't. I instructed her to try once every minute.

Servant's Devotion must have been the kind of ability that became unusable for a while after triggering it. I wanted to know how long that interval was.

"Um, I'm so sorry, my lord, for all the weird things I was thinking," Tarte apologized.

"It's fine, and I found it cute more than anything else. Still, we'll have to work harder on your mental training. You need to remove idle thoughts."

"Yes, my lord, I'll do my best!"

Although Tarte had superior focus in combat, she couldn't achieve that level of concentration in other situations.

"Your remaining skills are Spear Arts and Hard Worker. Both of those are pretty simple," I remarked.

"I've always believed Tarte was incredibly talented with a spear. This explains it," said Dia.

When I'd selected my C-Rank skill, I'd picked the versatile Martial Arts because I wanted to grow proficient with any weapon. It was a jack-of-all-trades, master of none situation, however. Going with a skill geared toward a single weapon ensured the best results with that armament.

"This is going to make me even more confident with a spear! Also, with a skill called Hard Worker, I have no excuse not to give everything my very best!" cheered Tarte.

I was positive that Tarte was destined to be a workaholic even without that skill.

"We have to decide what to do with your training from here on. Since you have Spear Arts, maybe it would be best if you ditched the gun and focused solely on your polearm," I suggested.

"I don't think we should do that. Guns' speed makes them convenient. When someone gets close to me, I can do this!" Tarte lifted her skirt and drew a firearm that was set in a holster on her thigh. It was a quick and elegant motion. Her training was clearly paying off.

"If you can draw it that swiftly, then perhaps you're right," I commented.

"Yes, my lord. If anyone gets too close for my spear, I can just grab this and blast them! Also, drawing my gun is much faster than putting my spear together, which is useful for sudden battles. Spears are also difficult to wield in narrow rooms."

Pistols had a limited range, but they were easy to handle.

"Hey, Lugh. This skill activates when she uses a spear, right? Why not make a spear that can shoot bullets?" suggested Dia.

"Would that even be a spear anymore? …It wouldn't be impossible. Might as well try it," I answered.

I decided I would base the design on a bayonet.

"Yes, please make me one!" exclaimed Tarte eagerly.

"Don't get your hopes up. It would be impossible to fold it like your current weapon, and its structure would make it brittle. It wouldn't function very well as a spear," I explained.

"Having access to long-range attacks would still be nice," said Tarte.

Tarte had the wind affinity, which didn't lend itself very well to offensive spells, and she wasn't incredibly competent at magic. As a result, Tarte couldn't fight from a distance. Perhaps she was jealous of Dia and me in that regard.

"All right, now we know all of your skills," I stated.

"We don't know yours yet, Lugh! You just learned our skills, so tell us yours," insisted Dia.

"Ah, I want to know what you have, too!" exclaimed Tarte.

Grinning, I explained that my skills were Rapid Recovery, Spell Weaver, Limitless Growth, and Martial Arts, plus the ones I had acquired from the hero.

"That's insane! How do you have one from every rank?! I've never heard of that before," Dia exclaimed with incredulity.

"I was fortunate," I responded.

"Wait, you didn't mention a D-Rank skill, my lord. I remember you told me once that everyone has a D-Rank skill," Tarte pointed out.

"That one's a secret… I'm keeping it for a surprise attack, and it will only work once. I've decided not to tell anyone about it," I explained.

The skill was worthless the moment people knew of it. Yet it was a perfect trump card so long as it remained undisclosed. Not even Dia or Tarte could be permitted to learn what it was.

"Oh, come on, keeping it private after we shared all of our skills is no fair. Now I *really* want to know," whined Dia.

"...Me too. But if you wish for it to remain secret, my lord, I won't ask," added Tarte.

They were both unhappy that I wouldn't confide in them, but I had my reasons.

"Okay, let's return to the estate. Maha sent us some delicious and interesting sweets from overseas," I stated abruptly.

"Changing the subject, I see."

"Wait, my lord!"

At last, we were aware of Dia's and Tarte's skills. Making effective use of them was going to push us to new heights. All that remained was to hatch Possibility Eggs. My investigation into that matter was progressing steadily. The time to start working on them was fast approaching.

For now, however, I decided I would enjoy some tea and sweets. Taking breaks was important, too.

Chapter 12 | The Assassin's Chocolate

After we finished with the appraisal sheets, I held a tea party. There was something that I wanted Dia and Tarte to try.

I chose to hold the little event at a table outdoors, where we had a view of my mother's so-called flower bed. It looked far more like a vegetable garden. Admittedly, after I'd seen the beautiful garden in the royal castle, this greatly paled in comparison.

"Some vegetables have flowers, too, so we may as well grow things we can eat." That was what my mother always insisted.

"I'm ready, you two," I announced.

I presented Dia and Tarte with a cup of special herbal tea each and lined the table with an item that was finally ready for sale after many long years of research.

Arranging things like this was typically a duty that fell to Tarte, but I wanted to surprise the girls this time.

"Hey, this is what you gave to me as a souvenir a few years ago. I remember thinking it was incredibly delicious and wishing you had more," remarked Dia.

"You have a good memory. That was a test run, but I've finally finished it," I responded.

Tarte's eyes widened slightly in remembrance. "Oh, I remember loving this, too! Lord Lugh let me taste test it once. It was bittersweet."

"Yeah, chocolate is so good," Dia said.

"It is!" Tarte added happily.

I had indeed laid out chocolate on the table. Soon, it would be Natural You's flagship product.

"Please try some," I offered.

"Wow, this is as delicious as I remember. It feels so luxurious," Dia commented.

Nodding, Tarte added, "Yes, it's enchanting. I don't know if I will enjoy another kind of treat ever again."

They both clearly appreciated it. I tried a piece as well and found it unsurprisingly delicious.

It possessed a smooth texture. I had achieved a perfect balance that gave you the taste of cacao without being too bitter. Back on Earth, this would have been called dark chocolate.

There was an undeniable air of luxury to it, and it was the best choice for demonstrating the chocolate's appeal.

"But compared to the chocolate you allowed me to try a while ago, the texture isn't as smooth, it's a little dry, and it doesn't taste as good. Ah, but it's still really, really delicious! Sorry for my rudeness," Tarte said.

"You don't have to apologize. I'm actually impressed you noticed that. This chocolate is definitely of lower quality than the variety I had you try before," I explained.

"Really? Did you use different ingredients?" she questioned.

"I'll explain later. Enjoy the chocolate for now."

"Yes, my lord!"

Evidently, Tarte's sense of taste had improved along with her cooking skill. It was impressive that she was able to notice the change.

"It goes perfect with herbal tea, too," remarked Dia.

"It's not bad, but I think coffee would complement it even better," I stated.

Dia cocked her head to one side. "What's coffee? I've never heard of it."

"I'll find some eventually. It has to be somewhere in the world."

Coffee was another commodity I'd been hoping to acquire. I would undoubtedly make an enormous profit if I brought it here.

"It took you a really long time to turn this into a product, my lord. You made the trial product back when we lived in Milteu," Tarte recalled.

"Yeah, it was a lot of hard work. Turning cacao pods into chocolate is challenging and time-consuming. I had to scout out and train an accomplished confectioner. After just under a year of trial and error, it's finally at a point where we can sell it," I explained.

The first thing you needed to do was extract the beans from the cacao pods, ferment them in banana leaves or something similar, and then let them dry.

That made it sound easy, but there were a lot of factors to consider. Yeast quality used in fermentation affected taste and texture, and the environment the beans were kept in required meticulous care. Fermentation rate changed depending on habitat.

There was also a trick to the drying, and even the slightest error ruined the whole process.

Once the beans were ready, you had to roast them, peel the shells, grind them, mix them with other ingredients, and refine the paste in a seventy-two-hour process called conching. Chocolate's smooth texture couldn't be achieved with brute force. Proper technique was necessary.

After all that, you had to temper the chocolate by heating and cooling it in a vessel over different temperatures of water to crystallize the fatty acids and improve the taste. That was the most challenging step and put the confectioner's abilities to the test. Once this process was complete, the chocolate could finally be molded and finished.

The confectioner I had recruited was an elite, but it still took him a year to earn a passing grade from me.

"It doesn't taste as good because someone other than Lord Lugh made it," Tarte speculated.

"That's exactly right," I answered.

"You truly are amazing, my lord."

Tarte then ate her last piece, her expression melting like chocolate. Dia finished hers as well, making much the same face.

They both clearly loved the sweet.

"Wow, we ate those fast," remarked Dia.

"...I should have savored them more," Tarte said with clear disappointment.

Both of their plates were empty. Usually, I would have seconds prepared, but I didn't have any extra to give the girls this time.

"Do you think this will sell?" I inquired.

"Heck yes! Nobles would pay their weight in gold for this stuff!" Dia exclaimed.

Bashfully, Tarte confessed, "I don't think I would be able to resist buying some if I could afford it with my allowance."

The taste wasn't the only reason they liked the chocolate. The polyphenols and theobromine found in cacao possessed a relaxing effect that healed fatigue. It wasn't just delicious, it was full-fledged medicine.

"I put the chocolate on the market and shipped some to regular customers last month, and it was received very well."

Sending gift baskets to regular customers encouraged repeat business and reduced crowding in stores, but the biggest advantage was sending items I wanted Natural You to stock to customers.

No matter how excellent the product, it would be meaningless if I couldn't get it in the hands of consumers. Making a gift basket was an easy way to do trial runs. I also only delivered them to those aristocrats with a major voice in society, who would spread the word for me.

Before long, rumors about chocolate began to spread like wildfire, coming to be known as the phantom candy.

"...You're going to get bombarded by angry customers," said Dia.

"This was the first time I've included sweets in the monthly shipment, but customers are always happy when I send them tea leaves. Why would they complain if I include some chocolate?" I questioned.

"No, no. They're going to demand that you sell them more chocolate and put it in stores," she clarified.

"You're right about that. I'm already receiving a ton of those complaints."

"I knew it."

Inquiries were pouring in daily. Everyone was asking if they could purchase more chocolate and when it would be available in stores. Honestly, the offers were starting to get ridiculous.

"If you consider those angry customers, then yeah, I've got a lot of them. Maha's been taking care of it," I explained.

Dia frowned slightly. "Wow, that sounds rough. Angry nobles are really annoying."

"Um, my lord, if your sweets are delicious and popular, won't other stores try to copy it?"

"Perhaps, but it won't be easy for them. Cacao pods are obtained from overseas. Natural You is the only company with a deal to import them, and chocolate is tough to make. If any competitors research the process, it will take them a century to figure it out."

Even if someone obtained a route to procure cacao pods, they'd never think to ferment the cacao beans in banana leaves.

"So we only have to worry about the confectioner getting bribed or kidnapped," Dia commented.

"I won't allow that to happen. I've invested a lot in this, so I've taken precautions. If anyone tries to get their hands on him… they'll regret it for the rest of their lives."

When I introduced moisturizer to the market, an appalling number of people had resorted to underhanded methods to discover its secrets. That experience had taught me how to deal with those kinds of situations. The major companies that went after Natural You last time met with some pretty nasty fates. I doubted anyone would try to steal my secrets again.

"Chocolate is so delicious but also such a handful," Tarte comment.

"That's what makes it a weapon. And in order to make it as strong a tool as I can, I've decided to put it on the shelves and send it to regular customers only once a month," I announced.

"What? That's evil. Making it so rare will turn it into a premium luxury," Dia said.

That was my goal.

Only Natural You could make chocolate, and knowingly making it a phantom candy would drive up its price.

Tarte, however, tilted her head in confusion. It looked like she didn't understand my reasoning for doing that. "Um, wouldn't it sell a lot even if it wasn't so rare? Wouldn't it be better just to make a lot of it?" she questioned.

"If I was only thinking about profit, then yes. However, the manufactured scarcity makes it valuable in other ways. Anyone would be delighted to receive some as a gift, for example. I made this chocolate expressly for that purpose. I can think of other uses as well," I outlined.

The more difficult something was to obtain among wealthy society, the more they desired it and the more jealous they would grow of others. Chocolate was perfect for that purpose. People who had tasted it would brag to others, spreading the word.

"Ah, that makes sense! I said that there would be many upset customers, but that's precisely what you want, right? You're planning on delivering people chocolate in exchange for favors they never would've given you otherwise," Dia concluded.

I nodded. "That's exactly right... Nobles love to show off, which makes them easy to manipulate. Especially those men trying to impress women. If they're desperate to get a lady some chocolate, they'll have no recourse but to obey my demands, whether they be for information or even some of their authority."

"Wow, that's dark. Darker than this chocolate!" exclaimed Dia.

No amount of money could earn someone an extra shipment of chocolate from Natural You. This was sure to produce incredible profits for the company in the future.

Surprisingly, the royal family of another nation had grown so obsessed with the confection that they'd made an absurd offer to procure more.

"That's why I'm going to use it as a gift when I visit people to make requests. It's already more valuable than gold among high society. I'm sure they'll do just about anything I ask."

I took out a box wrapped in elegant paper.

"You had more this whole time?! You could've given us seconds!" cried Dia.

"As I've explained, this is a gift," I responded.

"Who are you going to meet?" she asked.

"The person I know who has the light affinity. I want to make use of your skill. I'm sure you're itching to use light magic."

"Aw, man. I guess we can't have any, then…"

"I'll reward you both with an extra-large shipment of chocolate next time."

"Yay, I love you, Lugh!"

Dia hugged me while Tarte looked on jealously.

Tarte will never change, I guess, I thought, but then she surprised me by saying, "I love you, my lord," and embracing me, too. Perhaps she'd changed a little since activating Servant's Devotion.

After a bit, I said, "All right, please let me go. I need to prepare for the trip."

"Okay."

"Sorry, my lord."

Initially, I'd planned to only send Nevan Romalung a letter, but I changed my mind. Presenting chocolate myself was the best way to convince her to help. I also wished to discuss some things regarding the assassination of the prince that I couldn't bring up the last time we met.

With any luck, the chocolate would get Nevan to lower her guard. Sweets were mightier than the sword in the right circumstances.

Chapter 13 | The Assassin Sets Out

I was in my room, working on my plan to kill Prince Ricla. Since I was meeting Nevan in person, I wanted our discussion to be worthwhile.

I studied the prince's schedule that Duke Romalung had given me.

"Looks like the best time to target him would be the Founding Festival. Taking him out there will be easy."

The Founding Festival was held once a year to celebrate the creation of the kingdom. With demons about, there had been some discussion about not holding the celebration this year, but the notion had ultimately been discarded. The prince would be outside of the castle, participating in the parade.

The annoying thing about assassinating a prince was that there was no choice but to make it look like death from an illness. An unsolved murder of a royal would damage the kingdom's integrity. I would never be caught, of course, because I wasn't stupid. So those in charge would likely prepare a scapegoat.

That would make it hard to sleep at night, and I didn't know what kind of repercussions it would bring. There were a number of people in power who could abuse a prince's assassination to their benefit.

Death by sickness was another matter, however. There would be no need to find a criminal. It would also serve as a sufficient threat to Countess Granfelt and her followers.

"We can't afford to have them suspect he died of poison. That makes this a lot more challenging..."

I looked at a needle I had nearby. It was an assassination tool and laced with a toxin. The poison elicited some interesting symptoms, and an investigation would probably conclude that a victim perished to disease.

The problem was when to inject Ricla. If I hadn't needed to make it look like a sickness, I could've taken him down with a sniper rifle. Most people didn't know about firearms, and they'd never think someone could kill from over eight hundred meters away. It would be a cinch. However, circumstances demanded I get close.

The barrier around the castle is a problem.

If my target hadn't been royalty, I could've sneaked into their bedroom and killed them in their sleep. Unfortunately, that was impossible in the royal castle.

There was a magical field around the floor that the royal family lived on, and it activated when someone other than those of their lineage or the palace guards entered. It was a tool made by the gods that could sense the wavelength of a person's soul. I couldn't fool something made by deities.

I had confidence that I could slay the prince, hide, and escape even after the barrier was activated. However, the field's mere activation would make it obvious an intruder had been present. At that point, even if the prince's demise appeared to be due to an illness, they would rule it an assassination.

If I can't get out of the castle without being detected, I can't kill him.

"...It seems like Duke Romalung wants me to kill him at Mina's party, though. No, that might be a test."

According to the schedule, the prince would be attending a party sponsored by Countess Granfelt, the public identity of the snake demon Mina. It was positioned and written on the itinerary in a way that garnered attention.

The moment Ricla's death was proclaimed an assassination, the mission was a failure. However, if we framed the deed on the woman who'd bewitched the prince, that could change things.

If the prince was killed at Mina's party, we could make her into the scapegoat, enabling us to dispose of both the puppet and his master at the same time. There was no more efficient move... If the one pulling Ricla's strings hadn't been Mina, that is.

Under normal circumstances, if Countess Granfelt were accused of killing a prince, those she'd ensnared would distance themselves from her so as not to get involved. However, the second prince had been so thoroughly broken that Duke Romalung saw no other way than to end his life. Knowing this, I had to consider the possibility that Mina's numerous other pets might rebel in her name rather than break ties with the woman.

Duke Romalung was probably testing me. He wanted me to understand that drawing attention to Countess Granfelt would only be a bad thing.

"This is fun."

I would have to get through tight security at the Founding Festival, and I couldn't afford to leave any signs of my handiwork. It had been a while since my assassin's blood had gotten pumping like this.

This was a task beyond even the most elite covert killers. That was what made it so exciting.

Come next morning, a message arrived by carrier pigeon. It was Nevan's response to my request for a meeting.

"She wants me to come this afternoon…," I muttered.

That was awfully hasty. Surely the daughter of a duke was a busy woman. Making time for me couldn't have been easy, a testament to how highly she thought of me.

"Urgh… Lugh, that's so bright," complained Dia.

"Go ahead and get up. It's almost time for breakfast," I said.

The light from the window had roused Dia, and she sat up and rubbed her eyes. She wasn't wearing anything, so her adorable chest was bare.

"It's already this late? I didn't get enough sleep last night because you wouldn't let go of me."

"I think you've got that backward."

"You still don't understand the heart of a woman, Lugh. That's when you're supposed to just agree with me."

Dia slipped out of bed, walked over to the closet, and pulled out some clothes.

"It could be trouble if you ever let anyone see this closet. People might mistake you for a cross-dresser. Or curse you for having a harem."

"…I suppose so."

Both Dia and Tarte kept clothes and underwear in my room. Dia was my girlfriend and often slept with me. And whenever Tarte felt depressed over her family abandoning her, she would sneak into my bed.

When Dia finished changing, a knock came at my door.

Chapter 13

"Lord Lugh, Lady Dia, breakfast is ready!" rang Tarte's cheerful voice. Nothing announced the arrival of a new day quite like it.

After the morning meal, we climbed into a carriage and departed.

"Probably should've asked this earlier, but who are we going to meet?" inquired Dia.

"Nevan, the daughter of Duke Romalung," I responded.

"Wow, we're really off to see the Daughter of Light? I thought it might be her."

"What, have you heard of her?" I questioned.

"Of course. She's famous even in Soigel."

Nevan was both stunningly beautiful and possessed a rare elemental affinity. She was quite accomplished as well.

"I'm impressed you were able to get an audience with her," Dia admitted.

"...I guess I haven't told you yet. House Romalung is like House Tuatha Dé's boss. They decide if the requests from the royal family are in the country's best interest, then put them to use politically. This is top secret, of course," I explained.

Our public status and our secret jobs could never become intertwined.

So long as House Tuatha Dé's connection to House Romalung was kept classified, we could be disposed of on the small chance we were ever found to be a family of assassins. However, if our connection was common knowledge, House Romalung and perhaps even the royal family could be implicated if a Tuatha Dé was apprehended.

Dia thought on that for a moment. "Then is it okay for us to roll into their domain in broad daylight?"

"It'll be fine. I'm visiting as a Holy Knight on a job from the royal family. The contents of the mission explain our presence here. Still, I can't believe that House Romalung was able to set this up in just half a day."

The son of a baron's house entering the domain of a duke typically would've invited suspicion, but I was a Holy Knight.

"I'm nervous about meeting the Daughter of Light. I wonder what kind of person she is and if she's as beautiful as people say," Dia remarked.

"She was stunning," Tarte replied.

"Huh? Have you met? Oh yeah, you said that Duke Romalung and his daughter were present during the meeting with the princess." Dia's shoulders slumped gently.

Per the request to bring only one attendant, Dia had not joined us in the palace garden. She was still upset about being denied entrance.

After a while, we reached the domain of House Romalung. Our carriage rolled by extensive farmland, pastures, orchards, and even a city large enough to rival Milteu before we came upon our destination.

The journey took a considerable amount of time simply because of how vast this domain was.

"...Is this all truly one realm?" Dia wondered.

"They have everything you could imagine," Tarte commented with clear wonder.

"Most aristocrats find and polish one asset to support their domain while adding their own flavor to it. A domain with rich farmland might focus on exporting food. At the same time, one with a commercial city concentrates on trade. A region with a mining enterprise could develop an industry specialized in manufacturing. House Romalung, however, lacks that kind of narrow thinking. They are elite at everything—farming, livestock, manufacturing, commerce, and so on. That's why others sarcastically refer to them as the Romalung Empire. They are the most powerful nobles in Alvan," I explained.

House Romalung had been performing selective breeding and education geared toward creating the ultimate humans for hundreds of years, greedily gathering the most elite lineages and teachers from around the world. The result was a supremely skilled citizenry with unlimited knowledge and a network that extended into every conceivable area. This resulted in a society where the elite of the domain competed and pushed one another to advance further.

The region had achieved such immense prosperity that it had jokingly been dubbed an empire, but that title carried no small amount of fear with it.

When our carriage finally stopped, Tarte and Dia leaned out and went wide-eyed. I was astonished as well.

"Wow, that castle is amazing. It's so imposing," Tarte said.

"Yeah, *too* amazing! Can they get away with this, Lugh? This is greater than the royal palace. Is the king not upset about this? If a family did this in Soigel, they would get wiped out for their arrogance," Dia commented.

The Romalung castle was grander and more beautiful than any structure we had ever laid eyes on while also being extremely practical.

"This place was erected last year. It was built under the pretext of being the greatest structure possible by the current standards of technology. Its scale and functionality far surpass that of the royal castle... Creating something that eclipses the royal castle is hardly a way to make friends. However, it was tolerated because no one devotes themselves more to the crown than Duke Romalung," I detailed.

That was the official stance; more importantly, neither the royal family nor the other nobles had the strength to oppose House Romalung.

"So, Lugh. Just as a what-if scenario, could House Romalung take over the country if they wanted to?" asked Dia.

I nodded. "They've always been capable of that, even before I was born."

That was the truth of this country. Alvan was only able to remain as it was because of House Romalung's allegiance to the king. With their might, they could easily bring all nobles beneath their thumb, yet they elected to remain loyal to the crown.

"All right, let's get going. It's almost time for our audience," I called.

We crossed an elegant bridge built over a giant lake surrounding the castle. Scores of fish were visible through the clear waters, including species for consumption and decoration. The body of water acted as both a moat and a breeding farm. That was the kind of efficiency you could expect from House Romalung.

I braced myself. We were meeting with the monsters that ruled Alvan in their own den. If I got careless for a moment, we might be swallowed.

Chapter 14 | The Assassin Is Tested

We stepped foot into the most perfect castle in the kingdom. Actually, make that the world.

Just how much did this cost? What level of skilled personnel and labor made this possible?

It was scary just thinking about it.

"It's even more incredible up close," Dia said with wonder.

"Yeah," I agreed. "I've never beheld anything like this, and I doubt I will again."

This castle had a beautiful sense of aesthetics. Typically, when building a castle, you focused on functionality first and then added beauty and elegance later. However, while House Romalung had concentrated on performance, you could also tell they obsessed over every element, and the perfect capability of it all was radiant.

The unachievable luxury was enough to crush another noble's ambitions outright.

Dia's face lit up with curiosity. "Lugh, did you notice that?"

"Yeah, I sensed the mana. I can't believe they were able to construct such a complex magical tool."

When we passed through the gate, I got a feeling like we were being watched. We had crossed through a barrier capable of sensing people, like the one at the royal castle.

It was a cruder version, and I could've fooled it if I wanted to.

Even so, I was floored that human hands had created a magic tool with such complex functionality.

While I was brooding over that, we entered the castle and were greeted by a servant. He was a tall and graceful middle-aged man.

My heart skipped a beat when I saw him. I hadn't seen this face before, but I knew him.

What in the world is he thinking?

I expected the servant to lead us to a garden or a reception room. To my surprise, however, he ushered us to an indoor training ground. As was to be expected from the size of the castle, it was massive. Over two hundred swordsmen were crossing blades within.

"What do you think? These are House Romalung's most elite soldiers. Are they not impressive?" the servant asked.

I was flabbergasted. Every single fighter was a mage, and thoroughly trained. People with magic were supposed to be rare, but there were two hundred in this room alone.

House Tuatha Dé had twenty mages total among the main and branch families. That was including the elderly, women, and children.

Each of these mages was a strong, muscular man. The scale was incomparable.

How had they accomplished this?

The answer came without thinking. It could only be the result of House Romalung's unique methods. They had gathered remarkable people from every corner of the world to sire children with superior blood. Only the most elite were permitted to take the Romalung name formally, but many leftover people still possessed remarkable genetics, even if they couldn't call themselves Romalungs.

"Those are high-quality swords," I remarked.

"You have a good eye. We refer to those as steel swords here in Romalung," the servant replied.

Iron manufacturing technology was poor in this world, and most swords were cast with impure iron. These weapons were on another level, however. House Romalung had mixed iron with carbon to create the much stronger steel.

Their armaments were two steps ahead of the rest of the world. They also could not have made the steel into blades with simple casting. It had only been possible thanks to the talent they'd gathered from around the world.

They had two hundred mages using weapons that were leagues beyond what any other power had. There was no way anyone could challenge their strength.

"There is one more thing I would like to show you, Holy Knight. That group over there is made up of non-mages," said the servant.

"Those are bowguns," I observed.

"I am impressed by your knowledge."

The people in question were in the middle of firing practice, and watching was enough to send a chill down my spine.

The bowguns were a size bigger than standard ones. They were double-layered, which enabled rapid fire, and they had a foot pedal. Each had a winch to make drawing back the bowstring easier.

It was an evolved weapon that allowed the user to fire arrows with much greater force than would have been physically possible otherwise. Back in my old world, this would have been called a compound bowgun.

The user stepped on the pedal and then used their full body strength to draw back the arrow, from what I could see. That enabled much more power than pulling the arrow back with their hand alone.

On top of that, all of the men here were ridiculously strong, to the point that they looked like bodybuilders. They went red-faced as they planted their legs to draw out their full strength. Even relying on the winch, they could only barely nock the arrow.

"How much force do those bowstrings have?" I asked incredulously.

Achieving that level of tension should have been impossible with the world's current technology.

The two hundred people split into a pair of lines. Their target was a suit of steel armor about fifty meters ahead of them.

When an average mage strengthened themselves with mana, the hardness of their skin surpassed iron. An average mage could not, however, achieve the defenses of steel.

I understood now what they were demonstrating.

"You are about to see something quite interesting," the servant remarked with a laugh.

"Fire!!"

On command, the first row of soldiers loosed their bolts simultaneously. One hundred projectiles explicitly made for the bowguns lanced forward, piercing the steel armor.

It was proof that non-mages now possessed the ability to kill mages, something previously believed impossible.

"That was certainly interesting. This looks like the beginning of a new era," I commented.

Chapter 14

Truthfully, I was shocked. A mage's greatest asset was their abnormal defense. An arrow, sword, or hurled stone wouldn't do much damage when a mage was enveloped in mana.

That was why mages were unrivaled forces on the battlefield and the reason others could only defeat them with magic. They were the leading actors in battle and could kill as much as they wanted without risk to their own lives.

Yet that truth had just been upended.

No matter how strong or fast they were, mages would now perish as easily as anyone else. This development would reduce people with magic from invincible warriors to pieces with a unique strategic advantage like any other. A volley from one hundred soldiers would be very difficult to avoid.

Perhaps I was witnessing the end of the era of mages.

Of course, all of that was only if the mage in question was average. The best sorcerers could still handle such attacks. However, the majority of people with magic would lose their worth and influence.

I'd always known this would happen, but I had expected it to be when firearms and gunpowder came about. House Romalung achieving this level of might was unprecedented.

I took a deep breath. I was about done playing along with this facade. Intentionally, I changed my tone to one I would use toward a superior.

"For what purpose did you show this to me, Duke Romalung? Are you suggesting that you are going to war and that House Tuatha Dé had better join your side?"

Demonstrating overwhelming force to show that opposing you would be pointless was an established tactic for gathering allies.

"Ha-ha-ha, you saw through my disguise. That is embarrassing. When did you notice?" Duke Romalung answered. He was the servant.

"From the beginning. I am a professional. I will always see through amateur guises. First Lady Nevan tried to fool me, and now you."

"This is amateur to you? I felt rather confident about it."

The man put his hands to his face and pulled off his skin. He had been wearing an exquisitely made mask. Anyone other than me would have been fooled.

Tarte and Dia went wide-eyed with shock.

"To answer your question, I showed this to you because I would like you to wed my daughter, and I wanted you to see that the era of nobles will soon come to an end. It is only because of their overwhelming strength that aristocrats enjoy special privilege. Even the most incompetent feudal lord can stand above his citizenry if he promises them protection," the duke explained.

The greatest fool in the world could manage a domain so long as he possessed mana. Aristocrats held too much power for common people to oppose. Revolts were destined to fail before they ever began. The best an unhappy citizen could manage to do was run away in the night.

Citizens relied on their rulers for protection. They had no choice but to depend on nobles if monsters appeared. Thus, members of the ruling class were seen as gods, and people were willing to set aside any discontent if it meant surviving.

"That is true. If nobles can be killed easily, the whole system will turn on its head. There will come a time when possessing mana will be seen as no more than a talent like any other," I stated.

If regular people could easily kill mages and deal with

monsters on their own, then mages would come to be seen as simple humans rather than deities. All the pent-up frustration that had been building up over the years among the citizenry would explode, leading to insurrections in the domains ruled by the incompetent.

The same thing had occurred on Earth. Once knights could no longer overpower others, the nobility began to collapse.

Knights had been the strongest in society because of their specialized education, horses, and expensive armor. However, armor lost its purpose as weapons advanced, and their combat prowess became less helpful on the battlefield as well. Before long, knights couldn't even repel roaming brigands anymore. Once they became just another piece to be wielded in wartime, the respect, adoration, and worship the famed swordfighters had enjoyed vanished, and they became no better than anyone else.

A similar thing was beginning here. Incompetent feudal lords would likely get weeded out and replaced by commoners with no mana.

"Don't you find it funny? Talented people who have been ignored merely because they do not have mana will rise up one after another with newfound ambition... And they'll shove us, their former rulers, aside. Or perhaps they will create a country comprising only non-mages and try to eliminate us all," Duke Romalung stated.

"I don't think it humorous at all. The Alvanian Kingdom is currently at peace. I can't welcome outright war."

The duke sniffed at that. "It's not like you to say something so foolish." Calling such a logical statement foolish was very like him. He had his eye on the future.

"Allow me to guess what you're thinking. House Romalung

is now able to make weapons capable of killing mages. It's only logical, then, to conclude there's a chance others might be constructing them, too, and even if they're not, they eventually will. You want Alvan to deal with this change quicker than any other nation. If an army of foreign soldiers were to invade us as we are now with weapons that can kill mages, we would be ruined," I theorized.

"You are correct. That is not all, however," Duke Romalung replied.

"Furthermore, you believe one who possesses enough strength to survive these weapons is fit to rule. Someone like you, for example. No doubt your bowguns are not powerful enough to slay you."

Duke Romalung nodded, looking pleased. "Nor you. Yes, that was a perfect answer. There is not a single soul among my vassals who can see things from my perspective. I knew you were special."

An arrow traveling quicker than the speed of sound came flying toward me from behind. I caught it in my fingers without even turning around.

Duke Romalung applauded, then said, "With the introduction of these weapons, the nobles who hold power simply because they have mana will get sifted out. Any who survive will be the true nobles, the people worthy of leading this country. In that sense, you just earned a passing grade. I want you to join my family. However, I admit my methods of testing to see if you were worthy of my daughter were untoward, so I've prepared an apology."

"About that. I do not have any plans to marry Lady Nevan." That was something I would never have been able to refuse as a simple Tuatha Dé. As a Holy Knight, however, I could get away with it.

"I am aware of that. I still think you are best suited to my daughter, so please do. Don't worry, I won't do anything to upset you, and I won't try any tricks. Nevan is waiting for you, so go to her."

A real servant then appeared.

Duke Romalung claimed to be testing me, but in a way, this may have been his version of sincerity. He'd hoped to win me over by sharing his thoughts and intentions.

For a moment, I found myself thinking about how fun becoming the head of the Romalung family and ruling this domain would be. With such power, I could do anything.

Yet I was a Tuatha Dé. And I loved Dia and Tarte. I couldn't abandon all of that.

After a bit of a detour, I was finally going to meet with Nevan. Knowing her, she was plotting something. I couldn't let down my guard.

Chapter 15 | The Assassin Gains a New Ally

At last, it was time to meet the person I came for—Nevan.

It took more than being born as a direct descendant to bear the Romalung name. Using it showed that Nevan was the greatest masterpiece of her generation, one born from House Romalung's selective breeding and high education.

A servant was leading Dia, Tarte, and me to her.

"Hey, Lugh. What is light magic like? I don't know much about it because I've never seen it in practice, and it's difficult to find any documentation on it," said Dia.

"Ah, I am interested, too. It sounds really cool, but I've been wondering what it is actually like," Tarte added.

"It's more than just cool. It's an incredibly strong elemental affinity. When used for attack, it boosts your speed and firing range. As you might expect from the name, it enables you to move at the speed of light," I answered.

"That would make someone impossible to avoid," Tarte remarked, breaking into a sweat likely from just thinking about fighting someone like that.

"Yeah, you'd be done the moment they struck. I can't think of a deadlier attack," I agreed.

There was very little written on light magic, making the

subject challenging to learn about. Fortunately, I had been able to study it in the goddess's room.

Dia brought a hand to her chin. "You said 'when used for attack.' That means it has other uses, too, right?"

"Light magic can be used to search a vast area very quickly. It is capable of healing injuries as well. The best Tuatha Dé recovery magic can do is aid with surgery and natural recovery, but light magic is entirely different. It's capable of mending wounds on its own. Light magic is suited to just about everything," I explained.

"...Hearing that just makes me want it even more," Dia confessed, unable to contain her excitement.

If I had to pick only one elemental affinity, I probably would have selected light. There were two reasons I didn't, however.

The first issue was that light or dark had to be a person's *only* affinity. You could possess no others, and they were not included in Total Affinity. No matter how great light magic was, the collection of earth, fire, wind, and water was superior.

The second problem was the limited attack power. Light was swift, but its strength paled in comparison to fire's raw energy or earth's physical mass. I required the strength to kill the hero, someone with off-the-charts abilities, so any affinity with weaker punch was out of the question.

"This way, please," the servant beckoned.

He opened a door, and we heard the sound of a piano coming from inside. The melody being played was beautiful and elegant, much like the room itself.

The chamber was stocked with exotic items gathered from all over the world, yet the assortment lacked the tackiness of someone who had recently come into wealth. They were arranged with a sense of true nobility.

"Welcome, Lugh Tuatha Dé and friends. I've been looking forward to your arrival," Nevan greeted us. She turned around to look at us, her purple hair swaying as she did.

"I have also been looking forward to meeting you again, my lady," I responded politely.

"Aw, you flatter me. I remember your adorable retainer from last time. Who is the other girl?" she asked.

"Dia, introduce yourself," I instructed.

"I am Claudia Tuatha Dé, one of the Holy Knight's attendants. It is an honor to meet you," she said, bowing in the Alvanian style. Dia's conduct had reached an unrivaled level of grace.

"You are gorgeous, Claudia... I have a feeling we are cut from the same cloth," Nevan remarked.

Dia cocked her head to the side. "You think so?"

"Cut from the same cloth." Nevan sure was sharp. A mere glance was all it took for her to understand Dia was a high-born noble.

"Please be seated," said the Romalung girl.

"Thank you very much," I answered, doing as requested.

"When I heard you all were coming, I prepared some sweets that we had in reserve for the occasion. Yet you very kindly brought me something much, much better, so let us go with that instead. Ever since first tasting it last month, chocolate is *all* I've been able to think about. I thought I would never get any more."

Evidently, Nevan had heard about the chocolate I had passed to a servant upon entering the Romalung castle.

Politely, I replied, "I am glad to hear it pleases you."

"How did you manage to acquire chocolate? I tried my best to get some but had zero luck," Nevan questioned. Simply put, she wished to know how a lowly baron's son obtained something that a member of a duke's family could not.

"Ha-ha-ha, I think you know the answer to that already. I'm dating the proxy representative of Natural You. She grants me the occasional favor," I explained.

Nevan frowned. "Hey, using a personal relationship like that is cheating. It got me some chocolate, though, so I won't complain. Ah, here it is."

Servants carried plates beautifully arranged with chocolate and tea into the room.

"Nothing goes better with Natural You sweets than Natural You tea. I could never get enough of this elegant, bittersweet taste. Chocolate truly is unique—the perfect treat for the nobility. I wish I could eat it every day," Nevan said.

She stuffed her cheeks with the sweet like a child. As she was now, Nevan appeared no more than an overprotected daughter who knew little of the world.

It couldn't have been the real her, of course. This was likely an act she'd adopted because innocent behavior tended to delight men more than a serious, guarded personality.

I understood this precisely because of how perfect Nevan's acting was. Earlier, Nevan had said that she and Dia were similar, but one could say the same thing about her and me.

We made small talk as we enjoyed our chocolate.

"Have you given thought to my request regarding light magic?" I asked.

"Yes, I'd be happy to help. You are a Holy Knight, and you say you need it to defeat the Demon King and the demons. As a noble of the Alvanian Kingdom, how could I refuse?" she stated with a smile before producing a sheet of parchment.

There were magic runes written on it. In order for Dia to switch her elemental affinity, she required at least one formula of the appropriate kind.

"I appreciate it."

Yet as I reached out to grab the parchment, Nevan retracted it hastily. The lower half of the page was folded to keep it from being read in its entirety. Nevan had probably done that to prevent me from utilizing my photographic memory. The formula was a valuable asset to bargain over, but if I'd memorized the page's contents on sight, it would have been worthless.

"I will help you, but not for free," Nevan explained.

Raising an eyebrow, I inquired, "Was the chocolate not payment enough?"

"That did catch me by surprise. However, I wish another concession from you. Can you guess what it is that I desire?"

I immediately understood what she was after. She had been clear on that point the first time we'd met.

"I'm what you want, right?"

"That is correct."

"I'm afraid that light magic alone isn't worth trading my life to House Romalung. Surely you know that, too. I doubt you would find a man who could be bought at such a price worthy of being a Romalung," I stated.

"You are very good at this. When you word it like that, I can't even give you my backup proposal. I had thought that if you refused to marry me, I would at least request your seed," Nevan replied coolly.

Tarte and Dia, who were sitting next to me, both coughed. It seemed like that was quite a shock for them to hear.

Nevan was employing a textbook negotiating tactic. She was asking for something unreasonable first, then offering a compromise. It was a simple method but effective nonetheless. It left the other party feeling obligated to accept after rejecting the initial offer. Nevan, however, continued as though she had expected this outcome.

"Then how about this?" she began, clapping her hands together. "I want to know more about you. So...the next time you fight a demon, please take me along."

At that, she flashed me a wide smile.

"That would be difficult. I can't guarantee your survival. Naoise and his order of knights asked the same of me recently, but I refused them for being a burden. I can't grant you special treatment. It's better that you don't risk your life," I asserted.

"Your concern is unnecessary. After witnessing the duel between Naoise and your adorable maid, I can confidently say that I am stronger than her. I am a Romalung, after all."

Nevan couldn't have put it more convincingly than that. Her words were undoubtedly true. I had long since noticed that the girl sitting in front of me was a monster. She was definitely more powerful than Tarte.

I did have one point of consternation, however.

"You're joking about the duel, right? There's no way I wouldn't have noticed an intruder at that party."

"I promise I was present. Want to know how you didn't notice me? I switched places with one of Naoise's knights. I often serve as a body double, so I'm quite adept with disguises."

She got me.

I'd had no way of recognizing her, as the party was before I'd met Nevan. What's more, it was also my first time seeing Naoise's followers.

I had told Naoise at his party that if he was stronger than Tarte, he was qualified to fight with me. Now Nevan was holding me to that declaration.

"...Out of curiosity, what were you doing there? And why go through the effort of disguising yourself?" I questioned.

"Because I was interested in you... Well, that was only part of it. Truthfully, I attended because an idiot childhood friend of mine seemed like he might follow the same path as that blockhead prince. I wanted to keep an eye on things. I was grateful when you reprimanded him. That showed me how outstanding of a man you are and how useful you can be," Nevan explained.

"Naoise is a lucky man to be in the thoughts of a beautiful girl like you," I replied.

"I harbor no romantic interest in him. He's not worthy of being a Romalung, and I have no desire to bear his children. Naoise is more like a hapless little brother. He's always clung to me like a cute little puppy at every opportunity."

The daughter of House Romalung viewed the head of a class at the Royal Knights Academy as utterly innocuous. That was a terrifying thought. Naoise may have surrounded himself with some odd people, but he was undoubtedly a genius.

After a moment, I said, "Regarding your condition, I have to admit it's tough to swallow. I don't want to be responsible for anything that might befall you."

"If that is what you are worried about, then there is no reason not to let me come along. Standing in harm's way to protect the country is a noble's duty. Perhaps I could write a letter relieving you of blame in the case of my injury?" Nevan suggested.

"Why do you want this so badly?" I pressed.

"I don't appreciate you answering a question with one of your own. Yet for you, I'll oblige. I have two reasons. I find you so interesting, and I can't get you out of my head. Furthermore, I desire to know how you slew that demon as well as how you wiped out that horde of monsters during the attack on the academy. You are a man of many secrets."

"The answers are available in the report I submitted to the kingdom."

That document was top secret, and only a select few had access to it, but Nevan should have been one of them. There was no way she hadn't read the file already.

"Those reports are full of falsehoods. I want to see you in action with my own eyes."

My initial reaction was to refuse. For starters, I was concerned about what would happen if House Romalung learned about guns. I had just seen how capable they were at making weapons. If they started crafting guns, it might flip the country on its head.

Refusing Nevan would ensure she sent a lookout to pursue me. It was better to have her around.

"What's your other reason?" I asked.

"House Romalung needs your blood. I grow more certain of that every moment. If you had been a simple low-ranking noble, I could have coerced you into bed, but your status as a Holy Knight makes this more difficult. That is why I have decided to attack head-on and make you fall in love with me. I have to spend time with you so I can spark our steamy affair. Relax—it won't take long for you to become enamored with me. If seducing you does prove impossible, then I will just have you give me a child by force, so you have nothing to worry about. It will all be over before you know it."

Talk about confidence. And what was with that last bit? Is House Romalung truly so messed up, or is it just Nevan?

I felt Tarte's and Dia's piercing glares.

Clearing my throat, I said, "I have a couple of prerequisites of my own. You are not to speak a word of what you see when you're with me to anyone. You are also not to misappropriate my technology. If you can swear to do neither, then we have a deal."

"That is no problem. I look forward to fighting demons with you. Now then, here is the list of light magic spells."

Nevan definitely came out ahead on this deal, but I'd achieved my goal. Dia would now be able to use the light affinity.

There was one last matter to attend to, though.

"I prepared a document regarding my plan to assassinate the second prince," I stated. "The plan requires House Romalung's cooperation. This is as good a time as any to work out the details."

Without so much as glancing at the file, Nevan replied, "I approve of your plan. I'll look through it later."

"...Are you sure you should agree without reading it first?"

"You are not one to err when it comes to killing, are you? There's no way I would desire the child of a man who can't even do his job."

Evidently, Nevan put a lot of faith in me, although perhaps she trusted her own intuition, not me.

"I will make arrangements to become a Holy Knight attendant. I would like for you to request it from your end as well, Lugh."

With that, I had gained an unexpected companion. In time, she would prove to be a massive boon. So long as I didn't misuse her, she would undoubtedly be a powerful weapon, but one misstep could spell disaster.

Handling Nevan demanded special care, and that wasn't all. I needed to have a long conversation with Dia and Tarte later.

Chapter 16 | The Assassin Kills a Prince

We arrived in the royal capital. Our goal was to assassinate the second-eldest prince, Prince Ricla.

I'd collected information on the young royal while forming my plan. As I did so, I came to understand why Princess Farina and Duke Romalung considered him beyond saving. He had become a puppet for the snake demon Mina and didn't care in the slightest about his country.

Considering he'd been credited with unearned achievements while he served as Princess Farina's puppet, it wasn't astonishing to learn that Ricla was a bit dim. His lofty position as the second prince and his glowing reputation led to reckless behavior.

"*You didn't bring your adorable attendants,*" Nevan observed.

"*I wasn't keen on bringing you, either, if possible,*" I answered.

I was taking part in the Founding Festival disguised as a young merchant named Frank Hartman.

Frank Hartman was not one of the identities that my father had prepared, but rather one I had fabricated myself. The real man was a young peddler without any relatives who had been eaten by monsters while on the road, which made his name an ideal one to adopt.

A large number of stalls had been set up at the Founding

Festival. I opened one under my false identity. Nevan had decided to help run it for some reason. Naturally, she was also in disguise.

We were selling crepes. They were a special variety made with potato starch cooked into the batter, which gave the crepes an elastic texture. It also enabled them to be toasted lightly without crumbling and gave the batter near transparency.

The result was beautiful, and it felt great as it stuck to your mouth. Each crepe was filled with the highest-quality fresh cream and the finest in-season fruits.

I had hoped it would be a big hit, and sure enough, we had a constant line only moments after opening for business.

"*Getting a line in the royal capital where everyone has a refined palate is no small feat. It turns out you are an elite chef, too. Still, doesn't it seem like we're doing too well?*" Nevan asked.

"*Selling anything less than top-rate would actually cause us to stand out more. A stall permitted to operate in the royal capital needs a product to match,*" I responded.

It was normally better to have as few people around as possible when assassinating. The more witnesses there were, the more difficult things became. That was the standard way of operating, anyhow. For this assassination, a more significant number of customers would make it easier to work without drawing attention to myself.

Nevan considered my answer. "*That is true. But won't that be disadvantageous to your main purpose here?*"

"*I can operate fine under these circumstances. The stall being this busy makes for a good cover.*"

No one would suspect that the one running a stand with so many customers was responsible for a murder.

Nevan and I conversed soundlessly by reading each other's lips and barely moving our mouths. Furthermore, we were only eyeing the other out of the corners of our eyes. Staring at someone's lips without saying anything would have appeared conspicuous.

This was a special technique, but Nevan had mastered it after I taught her one time. She was a true monster.

I'd had to leave Tarte and Dia behind because they weren't yet capable enough with disguises. If it had only been a matter of appearance, I would have found a way to make it work.

However, neither girl possessed sufficient skill to mask her personality. To perform another identity to perfection, you needed to construct that person within yourself. Breathing, habits, speech, gestures, way of thinking, how you interacted with people, and more, all of it needed to be changed and maintained at a subconscious level.

Anything less meant you were doing nothing but wearing a costume. It was not something you could learn in a day. Yet Nevan had already perfected the art. It made sense. She did serve as Princess Farina's body double, after all.

"*I'm looking forward to seeing how you kill him,*" she chirped.

"*I gave you the document outlining the plan,*" I responded.

"*I read it, but all you wrote was that you're going to make it look like he died of illness. You sure like to hold your cards close to the vest.*"

"*Just relax and watch. I'm not sure you'll understand even if you do, though.*"

This job was 90 percent complete the moment I'd secured this spot. I'd conducted extensive research on the route the royal family planned to take during the parade, what time they would pass each point, the number of guards and their stations, the carriages that would be used, and more.

This is the most accessible location to kill him from.

There was one point on the route where the road grew narrow and curved, meaning the prince's carriage would have no choice but to draw quite close to the spectators.

Our crepe stall was on that spot. The prince's carriage would come within three meters of it, and that was near enough to assassinate Ricla while making it seem like an illness. House Romalung had aided in securing this place.

The crepes were continuing to sell well.

Once the parade got underway, the number of customers waned slightly.

Some soldiers stepped forward and altered the direction of our line to ensure the procession had room to pass through the narrow street. Carriages with members of the royal family then began to pass by one after another.

The firstborn prince was exceptionally popular. His military prowess was praised as being godlike, and he was an able combatant in his own right. However, his sense for politics was lacking.

The next to draw loud cheers from the crowd was Princess Farina, the client for this assassination. People loved the young woman for her breathtaking beauty and her lovely smile.

Once a month, she sang at a charity concert in the largest hall in the Alvanian Kingdom, and it was a packed affair every time. Tickets sold out in minutes. Every attendee swore she had the voice of an angel.

Farina's popularity was akin to a pop idol, but that was a front for her true nature as a master tactician.

All of the other princes and princesses except for Ricla passed by uneventfully. They weren't all that popular. People didn't view

Chapter 16

them as special beyond their having been born into the royal family.

"Here he comes."

The second prince brought up the rear of the parade. The two biggest stars had been given the opening and closing acts, so to speak.

In total contrast to the first prince, Ricla was praised for his many accomplishments in politics and diplomacy. He was also good-looking and enjoyed fame on par with his older brother and Princess Farina.

The throngs of people roared excitedly as Prince Ricla came into sight. A cheerful smile was on his face. His voice was high and spirited, and he looked as handsome as every portrait depicting his visage. There was no life in his eyes, however. His gaze appeared unfocused and sluggish. It was clear to me that he wasn't in his right mind.

I looked at him with my Tuatha Dé eyes and analyzed the color and wavelength of his mana.

Mages were always subconsciously enveloping themselves in magical power, even when they weren't on guard. That was why if a regular person tried to stab a mage with a sword, they would not be able to inflict a fatal wound.

Killing a mage required considerable force. Yet any attack with that necessary firepower would expose me immediately.

He couldn't be killed without firepower, but any level of firepower would make it detectable that he was assassinated.

Right there.

I began an incantation. I only barely moved my lips and spoke at a volume that not even the customers waiting for crepes right in front of me could hear. This was a new spell that Dia and I had developed.

It was a non-elemental spell designed to eliminate mana. By firing magical power that matched the target's wavelength, you could open a hole in their protective mana armor. It didn't inflict any physical damage, which left the recipient unaware they had been struck.

Casting it wasn't easy, however. It was impossible to know a person's wavelength unless you possessed Tuatha Dé eyes, and using too much power risked piercing through the target's armor rather than simply erasing it, which the target would feel.

I finished the recitation just before Prince Ricla reached us, launching an invisible bullet of mana toward his neck and opening a hole in his shield. I then used an assassination tool disguised to look like equipment for my stall to shoot a needle. The piece of equipment was large enough that opening a booth had been the only way to reliably conceal it.

The second prince grabbed his neck, then turned and spoke to his guards. I couldn't hear them over the crowd, so I read their lips.

"What is it, Your Highness?"

"I just felt a prick. It's nothing. Keep moving."

The prince removed his hand from his neck. There wasn't a mark. My job had been a success.

Ricla passed by as if nothing had happened.

"Here's your crepe, good sir," I said, passing a customer their order with a grin.

As far as anyone knew, I was only cooking crepes. I was sure that not a single person noticed I had just killed the second prince.

Once the parade ended, an announcement proclaiming the end of the Founding Festival sounded.

The stalls began to close, while drinking establishments zealously called out to potential customers.

Nevan and I quickly finished cleaning up our booth.

"Phew, I'm tired. I'm happy our crepes were so popular," Nevan remarked as she stretched.

"Yeah, me too. Let's return to the inn," I responded.

It would look strange if two ordinary merchants left the city so late in the day, so we'd secured lodgings in advance. Nevan was, of course, still disguised as a clerk for my stall, and I would remain as Frank until departing the capital.

"It's just the two of us at the inn, and you are far from home. This is the perfect chance for you to cheat on your little girlfriend. I won't say a word," Nevan proposed.

"I don't feel like it. Stay out of my room," I stated curtly.

Undeterred, Nevan suggested, "I've been thinking. It would be perfectly natural for two young and spry merchants to celebrate their profits by enjoying a meal at a nice restaurant."

"...Yeah, you have a point. Let's go," I agreed.

"Wonderful. Show me where the rabble like to eat."

Eateries in the royal capital were expensive across the board. That Nevan could refer to them as the restaurants of "the rabble" was precisely what made rich people so terrifying.

Chapter 16

When we were at the Royal Academy, the capital was pretty much the only place we could go for fun, so I was familiar with a few spots in the city. I picked one with private rooms and good food. I wanted one where we could be alone because I figured Nevan wished to talk.

After our orders arrived, I used a wind spell to prevent our conversation from being overheard. Nevan saw that and smiled, evidently understanding what the magic did.

"Good work out there. I have a few questions. Is it okay that the prince didn't die?" she asked.

"He will in time, Lady Nevan. In his own room in the castle. That will cause the least trouble," I answered.

I had Ricla's schedule memorized, and I'd adjusted the dose of poison so that he would perish after returning to his chambers.

"Aw, what's this 'Lady Nevan' stuffiness? I prefer it when you speak casually."

"I don't need to act as Frank right now."

I was isolating the sound of the room using wind magic, and we were speaking of the assassination. Thus, I was Lugh, not Frank.

"Exactly how did you kill him?"

"I used a needle. It was only a few millimeters long. I installed a machine disguised as cooking equipment in the stall to fire it. Shooting such tiny projectiles is difficult, so I had no choice but to use a large device. Opening a stall was the only way to bring in the contraption and conceal it while also getting within striking range of the prince."

Our crepe booth truly had been the perfect facade.

"You can kill someone with a needle that small?"

"Yes, though it would've been impossible using a normal one. The needle itself was solidified poison. I shot it into a vein on his neck so that it would be carried through his bloodstream to his heart, where it will melt."

"And what happens then?"

"It will cause his muscles to relax. After his heart slows, his blood flow will stop. He will suffer a cardiac arrest, making his death look like an illness."

"Won't they discover the poison?"

"The needle will melt, and all the toxin does is relax muscles in the body. There won't be anything left to find."

Truthfully, there would be traces left in Prince Ricla's body, but nothing in this world could detect them.

"What an interesting poison. I've never heard of anything like it."

"In a few hours, the prince will retire to his room, where he is guarded by an artifact that keeps out intruders. He will then die of a heart attack. It will appear as nothing more than death from sickness."

"Hmm-hmm, how perfect. That's a wrap on this issue. We'll make great use of this killing method in our future work," Nevan stated with a captivating smile before taking a sip of her alcohol. That was all she did, but somehow, she made the gesture seem tremendously alluring.

"That was a great meal. How about we head back?" I suggested.

Nevan nodded. "Yes, let's." She offered her hand, silently telling me to escort her.

I could allow her that much. Our success today was due to her groundwork and presence at the crepe stall. I needed to express my gratitude.

Still, I couldn't afford to get careless. Nevan was already trying to entice me by pressing her chest against mine. It was also obvious she wasn't wearing a regular perfume, but one designed to arouse men.

Now that I thought about it, her every mannerism was chosen specifically for that purpose. She was doing everything she could to break me down.

"The night is young," she said with a giggle.

Apparently, the real battle would begin once we got to the inn. I could not allow myself to lose. Maha and I had a date the next day, and arriving with the scent of another woman on me was a bad idea. Maha worked hard for me, and she didn't deserve that.

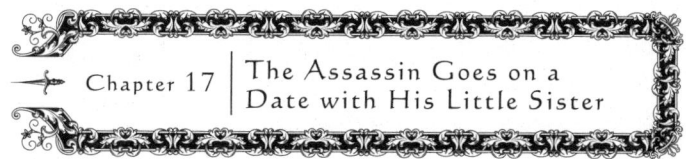

Chapter 17 | The Assassin Goes on a Date with His Little Sister

I was staring out of the window while eating breakfast at the inn.

The royal capital was in a frenzy after the announcement that Prince Ricla had died of sickness. Newspapers had recently come about thanks to the development of printing technology, and a special edition detailing the second prince's demise was flying off the shelves. I had a copy in front of me.

I sipped some fruit juice while reading.

"It's bad manners to read a newspaper while eating, and it's rude to the girl you're with," Nevan chided. We were still in disguise.

"I'm working. I need to check how they reported the prince's death," I answered, speaking with Frank's casual tone.

"Men are always hiding behind their work. I do love the capable sort, though."

"I don't need your flattery. Want to head out? I want to get to the next town before long."

"That wasn't flattery," Nevan replied with a sigh. "This is humiliating. I tried all night to seduce you, but you didn't lay a hand on me."

"Starting to hate me yet?"

"No, my passion for you burns brighter than ever."

"That's too bad."

I had no reason to dally here. It was time to depart.

We left the royal capital by carriage and traveled to a neighboring settlement. Upon arrival, we headed toward the designated inn and turned over our carriage and luggage upon arrival.

Duke Romalung would take over the case from here and destroy all evidence. This place we were staying at was one of House Romalung's bases.

I changed my clothes and entered another room. Nevan, now back to her radiant self after removing her own disguise, was waiting there with Duke Romalung.

"Excellent work, Lugh Tuatha Dé. I trusted you would be able to pull it off, but this was brilliant. Absolutely incredible. I'm impressed by how convincingly you made it look like a natural death. No one even suspects assassination."

Duke Romalung had also been in the royal capital yesterday. The heads of the four major dukedoms always gathered for the Founding Festival. As such, he knew how the higher-ups were handling the second prince's sudden demise.

"That must mean that death by illness isn't just the public stance; it's what the top brass in the government believe as well," I said.

Sometimes, a government would report that a death resulted from sickness even if they knew it was an assassination to keep the public from panicking. I had seen that kind of thing happen a lot.

"That's correct. He had no external wounds, there were no traces of poison, no intruders in the royal castle, and he suffered a heart attack in his private chambers. Foul play seems all but impossible. Did your knowledge from the public Tuatha Dé profession enable you to kill him this way?" the duke inquired.

"It did. No one understands how to kill better than doctors. They're also the ones who determine the cause of death," I answered.

"That is equal parts enlightening and terrifying. If you felt like it, would you be able to make it look like even I died of illness?"

"Under the right conditions, yes. But I would never. We Tuatha Dé wield our blades only for the sake of the Alvanian Kingdom, and the country needs the Romalungs."

There was a lot about them that rubbed me the wrong way, and they tended to do whatever they pleased, but there was no doubt they put the nation's best interest first.

"What an exemplary answer. Heartfelt, too. I knew I liked you. You continue to grow greater in my eyes. I'll send your reward through the usual route, so please look forward to it. I added a little something extra this time," said Duke Romalung.

"Then, if you'll excuse me, I am going to head out," I announced.

"Wait a moment. I want to ask you something first. It's a dire matter." Duke Romalung spoke calmly, but there was an edge to his voice that brooked no refusal. I had stood to leave, but this stopped me in my tracks. "How long will it be before I get to see the faces of my grandchildren?" he asked.

What a stupid question.

"I wouldn't know," I responded flatly.

"...I see. That is disappointing."

"I'm sorry, Father. I tried my absolute best, but the disguise must have halved my charm. He didn't lay a finger on me," Nevan apologized.

"So that's what happened. After hearing that Nevan failed to seduce you, I admit I wondered if you were homosexual. Hmm, so you will begin your efforts anew when the academy reopens, Nevan?"

"Yes, I guarantee I will find a way to become pregnant with his child during our next semester."

His daughter is even worse.

Still, Nevan's mentioning of the academy reminded me that, according to the newspaper, restoration on the building was progressing rapidly. The reopening was scheduled for next month.

"Okay, I'm really going now," I insisted.

"Good luck on your date," remarked Nevan.

"I don't think I ever mentioned that to you."

"It's obvious just by looking at you." Nevan was acting clever, but some servants had likely done an investigation on that matter for her. "Also, I expect my idiot childhood friend is going to cause some trouble. But please remain his friend," she added.

Idiot childhood friend?

It took me a moment to recall that Nevan had referred to Naoise that way. She was worried enough about him to go through the effort of disguising herself and sneaking into his party. Undoubtedly, she was still monitoring him. Perhaps she'd even discovered something.

"Don't worry. I won't abandon him," I assured her.

Precisely what was Naoise getting involved in? I left for my date with more than one thing to fret about.

◇

Chapter 17

After departing the inn, I made for the restaurant where Maha and I were supposed to meet. A merchant I trusted had recommended the place, so I had high expectations.

The eatery maintained a trendy feel. It was pricey, but it felt less like an establishment for rich people and more like a place for ordinary folks to eat when they wanted to splurge. This resulted in a warm, casual atmosphere.

I told them the name of the party I was meeting, and I was led inside.

"You're right on time, dear brother."

"Long time no see, Maha."

Natural You had also participated in the Founding Festival, so Maha had been in the royal capital, too.

We ordered some tea and cookies to snack on as we talked.

"You get prettier every time I see you," I complimented her.

Her lustrous blue hair was so dark that it appeared nearly black. Although Maha's chest wasn't big, she possessed a perfect figure. Today, she was dressed stylishly and wore light makeup.

Unlike Tarte and Dia, whom I would consider cute, Maha was best described as beautiful.

"Yeah, and you have no idea how many pests I get following me around as a result. It's rough. I need some insect repellent," she lamented.

"Have you considered hiring a bodyguard?" I suggested.

"There is a more cost-effective option, you know. I would be thrilled if you gave me a band for the ring finger on my left hand."

"I'll think about it."

Maha enjoyed teasing me, but that hadn't been a complete joke. Whether or not it was for her ring finger, I was sure it would make her happy if I sent her jewelry. I decided to find a nice piece for her.

"I'm impressed you were able to make time to meet me," I said.

Looking exasperated, Maha explained, "It wasn't easy. I had to push myself to do it. Truthfully, I'm exhausted. I've barely slept the last few days. As soon as I arrived in the capital, I was flooded with requests to form a partnership, offers for technological assistance, demands to open new branches, deals for support if I broke from the Balor Company, and so on. They were all after Natural You's products."

"Natural You is still the only company that knows how to make moisturizer," I pointed out.

"That goes for chocolate now, too, and our numbers have soared for it. Just recently, I got a letter from the third prince explaining that the royal family had received demands from a foreign noble house that included a request for a gift basket containing moisturizer and chocolate."

"So we're serving the royal family now, huh?"

"It's such an honor I could cry."

Maha and I both laughed.

She was the proxy representative of the cosmetic brand I had created, Natural You. The company's secret to success was selling attractive products that no one else could make. Primarily, we focused on items from Earth that I remembered how to create, were difficult to reproduce, and would earn a significant profit.

"What happened next?" I questioned.

"I requested enormous compensation," Maha answered, outlining what she had asked for.

"That's wicked. I'm impressed you got them to agree to that."

"It was easy. I identified the foreign aristocrat who sought Natural You products, and I found out what they present to the kingdom. Then I merely appealed for the highest possible price the royal family would still be willing to meet. The royal family knows that there are many influential people among our customer base. They don't want to put undue pressure on Natural You. I surmised that they would yield if I gave them a price just within their range."

Maha had employed a standard mercantile tactic. Information meant everything in a negotiation. Victory was assured when you knew how much your opponent was willing to compromise.

With our business concluded, Maha and I chatted about a variety of things. She spoke to me very cheerfully, and it became apparent that she wanted me to applaud her efforts. I met that desire by listening attentively and enthusiastically praising her at every opportunity.

Her eyes were shining, and she nearly talked herself hoarse. Maha was a very mature girl, but she tended to act more her age at times like this. She really was an adorable little sister.

Watching Maha act so excited wound up making me feel happy, too.

"You've been working hard," I stated.

"That I have. I'm doing my best. That goes for your secret efforts as well. I've been looking into Countess Granfelt and Naoise, just as you requested," she responded.

Maha handed me some files. I had asked her to look into Countess Granfelt, the false identity of the snake demon, for obvious reasons. I'd added Naoise to the job out of concern for him.

"If House Romalung is already cooperating with you on this, why did you go out of your way to seek my help? Couldn't you have just left it to them?" questioned Maha.

"My information network and theirs are equal in scale, but

they're of different varieties. Two investigations on the same target can produce different results when performed from a different angle."

House Romalung conducted professional research using intelligence agents.

I used similar operatives, but they were civilians who focused primarily on marketplace rumors, the flow of money and goods, and other types of knowledge that merchants had a unique eye for.

"...Thank you. I get the picture. I would never have thought Naoise might cast aside his knightly honor," I said.

Despite having promised not to involve himself with Countess Granfelt after losing the duel, he still had. It was difficult to believe that the prideful Naoise would sully an agreement that he'd staked his honor on, but the investigation results couldn't be denied.

"Yeah, though he doesn't seem to have been bewitched like the second prince was," Maha added.

"That worries me. The first thing I'd suspect upon learning Naoise had abandoned his principles would be a love affair," I remarked.

What was he hoping to achieve by getting close to that demon?

An image of Naoise's face suddenly appeared in my mind. It was the expression he'd made after losing his duel to Tarte.

"Tell me! Tell me how you obtained that strength! I need... To grow stronger..."

His words hadn't been born from desire. They felt more like the pleading of a man at his wit's end. Was that why he'd gone to Mina?

That didn't make sense, though. It felt unlikely that Naoise knew of Mina's true identity. Even if he did, was he truly willing to become an enemy of humanity just for strength?

My eyes caught a particular line in Maha's report. "...It says here that he disappeared."

"Yes, he reportedly told his acquaintances and family that he was leaving on a training trip. Countess Granfelt vanished at the same time," Maha explained.

"Do you think that was a coincidence?"

"Probably not."

What in the world was Naoise thinking?

Nevan had asked me to remain Naoise's friend despite whatever trouble he caused. That concerned me, too.

"Do you mind looking into where Naoise is now?" I questioned.

"I already am. Our agents will contact me right away if Naoise shows up in a town within the Balor Company's distribution network," Maha replied.

"You're so good at this it's scary."

"You *are* the one who trained me, dear brother... I work hard because I want to be helpful to you, even if this is all I can provide."

Just like Tarte did occasionally, Maha tilted her head, asking for a pat. I did as she wished, and her calm expression melted into that of a pampered child. I was probably the only person in the world who got to see this side of her.

"All right, our work is done. What do you say we begin our date proper?" I suggested.

The trouble with Naoise was worrisome, but there was nothing to be done at the moment. Maha had done a lot for me recently, and I wanted to make her happy.

"Yes, let's. I've been looking forward to this day for a long time," she responded.

I picked up the receipt and stood.

"What fun activities do you have planned this time?" Maha asked.

"That's a secret."

"I like it when you take the lead because I always discover something new. Lugh, I've meant to ask this for a while. Isn't it about time to finally upgrade me from little sister to little sister and girlfriend?"

"...You're family, Maha."

"Wow, I'm surprised. I've made more progress than I thought. You usually answer immediately, but this time, you had to think for a second. Perhaps you've had a change of heart? I'll have to press you further on this," she said with a giggle. Then she jovially put her arm around mine.

I was taking the lead on this date, and I had made thorough preparations to reward Maha for her hard work.

My only focus for the rest of the day was to show Maha a fun time.

Chapter 18 | The Assassin Keeps an Ally in Check

While eating dinner with Maha, I couldn't help but think that dates were fun.

Spending time with Dia and Tarte was amusing, too, of course, but Maha's dates differed in key ways.

Dia would give herself entirely to my lead and voice various demands throughout the date.

Tarte also left the decision-making entirely to me. Unlike Dia, however, she would watch my mood and give me meticulous care, never acting on her own desires. She would even pretend to enjoy the date for my sake, even if she had no interest in whatever we were doing.

Maha and I, on the other hand, would take turns taking point, and she would actively come up with ways to give me a fun time.

I'm not saying that dates with the other two were boring, of course. Dia's self-indulgence was cute, and the directness of her demands made it easy to know what she wanted to do.

Tarte's tendency to fake like she was having fun made things a little difficult, but her behavior proved how much she loved me. The concern she displayed throughout our dates was a little embarrassing, but it was nice at the same time.

In short, all of them were fun in unique ways.

"Today's date was so great… I really hate that I already have to go," Maha said with a sigh.

"I had fun, too. I guess we'll see each other again at the next party," I replied.

"That's right. It's the last one I couldn't turn down. I've had enough of the royal capital. All the bigwigs have too much time on their hands," she complained.

The aristocracy had become enthralled with Natural You. Upon learning that Maha was coming to the royal capital, every noble in the city invited her to a social function. They did so partially out of a desire to obtain Natural You products before anyone else and learn more about the brand… But most of all, they wanted to brag to others about having Maha at their party.

"I've been considering something for a while now. I hardly ever act as Illig anymore… I think it would be a good idea to remove the *proxy* from your title and make you the true representative of Natural You," I stated.

Illig Balor was another name of mine, a son of the distinguished Balor Company.

"I don't want that," Maha answered immediately.

"You already have the position in all but name. Your job would become a lot easier if it was official," I protested.

"I understand that it would be beneficial from a management standpoint. I'm often reminded of how differently people view the titles of representative and proxy representative when I'm in negotiations," Maha remarked.

I was the Natural You brand representative, but Maha's authority was technically no different than mine. That wasn't how people saw it, however. They would always think of Illig Balor as the person in charge of the brand and Maha as a mere substitute.

"Then why not? Are you holding back for my sake?" I questioned.

"That's not it. I just like working below you, dear brother. I want to labor for you, and I'm not interested in letting go of anything that connects us, no matter what it is. That is my selfish desire. I want to remain your Maha until the end."

"That doesn't sound like a merchant. They always prefer to have their own store over working for another. Most dream about starting their own enterprise."

"...I have that dream, too. A dream of growing as a merchant, saving money, collecting my scattered friends, starting a new business, and taking back the company that was stolen from my father."

"You could see it all accomplished if Natural You was yours."

Maha smiled boldly. "I'd rather you didn't underestimate me. I can make that happen even without owning Natural You. Actually, I'm very close to achieving it already. I sent you a report. The new people I've hired are all performing very well."

"That's true."

Maha had been an orphan before she'd met me, and she had run a business together with others like herself. Those days came to an end when her group was split up and placed into orphanages throughout the city.

Recently, Maha had been searching for her old comrades and hiring them on as Natural You employees. Although she did so partially for personal reasons, it was also to the company's benefit.

Maha's old friends had grown tough from their harsh lives. Maha had led them, but the orphans had still run a successful business as children. They possessed valuable experience.

The children that Maha had recruited were easily outperforming our investment in them. Natural You had gained some gifted personnel.

"I've also been able to split my father's former business to a third of its original size. I showed you my acquisition plan, right?"

"You did."

Maha's father's former company had been suffering ever since the new owner took over. Lately, it had even started selling off assets.

Maha was acquiring stores her father's old business put on the market and was turning them into Natural You branches.

I once told Maha, *"I won't tell you to keep personal feelings out of this, but if you decide to follow your heart, make sure you succeed."*

She had done exactly that.

"I can achieve my dream while remaining under you. I'll save my former colleagues, reclaim my father's company, and support you. Don't tell me to choose one. I'll take it all. That is how skilled I am, and that is why I can remain in my current position," Maha declared.

I smiled. She really was tough. Her strong affection also moved me.

"Thanks, Maha."

"You're welcome. At first, I felt like I owed you. If you had never adopted me, I would have either been killed or sold off to some perverted noble. You saved me and allowed me to grow as a merchant. That was why I always thought I needed to repay my debt to you."

"And now you think differently?"

"Not exactly. I still feel like I owe you. But more than that,

Chapter 18

I'm working hard simply because I love you, dear brother." Maha beamed. Her expression radiated happiness and satisfaction.

My heart began to pound. I was reminded once again that Maha was no longer a child, but a beautiful woman.

"I love you, too, Maha."

"I know... Still, it's frustrating that it never goes further. With how well things went today, I thought we might have gone all the way. I really need to leave. Give me my goodbye kiss, dear brother."

Maha stood and waited expectantly with her eyes closed.

I was unduly aware of her long eyelashes, beautiful skin, and the smell of her body mixed with her light perfume.

Letting that emotion carry me, I kissed Maha on the lips. When I broke away, her face went red, and she pressed her hands to her mouth.

"...Thank you. Normally, when I ask for that, you give it to me on my cheek or my forehead."

"I felt like this was more fitting today."

"Hee-hee, I'll do my best at work!" Maha said excitedly with a smile before running out of the restaurant.

Seeing her dash off like that was rare. She must have stayed with me until the last possible second.

I decided to order some herbal tea to help me calm down. As I was enjoying the beverage, someone made a noise to get my attention before sitting down in front of me.

It was my newly gained ally.

"You're so popular with girls. The cute little sorceress, the big-chested lance-wielding maid, the fake princess, and now that beautiful merchant. They're all so adorable and talented and head over heels in love with you."

Chapter 18

"Mina. I had no idea you were in town."

It was the snake demon, the criminal responsible for dominating the prince whom I had to kill yesterday. Why was she here, and how did she know where to find me?

Perhaps I had an information leak. I would need to investigate that later.

"I'm pretending to be human because I want to enjoy your culture. There's no way I would miss a festival. Oh, it was *so much* fun! I don't know how humans can create something so wonderful despite being so small, frail, and ugly. It just warms my heart."

It amazed me that Mina could consider infiltrating the depths of noble society as Countess Granfelt to be mere amusement.

"Did you come here to make small talk?" I demanded impatiently.

"Truthfully, I'm shocked. You really got me. You broke my plaything. That was my second-favorite one," Mina lamented.

"What are you talking about?"

That was a leading question. I wasn't stupid enough to give Mina evidence of my assassination.

"Oh, we're playing dumb, are we?"

"I honestly had nothing to do with it. I am a noble with undying loyalty to the Alvanian Kingdom. I would never so much as point my blade at the second prince."

"Is that your roundabout way of demanding proof? I don't have anything of the sort, dear. However, I do make an effort to maintain the health of my playthings, and that one should not have collapsed. Thus, I can only conclude that someone hurt him. The only person in the world who could have made it look like he died of an illness under the circumstances is you. That means you killed him."

"That's quite the leap in logic."

"Yes, I know that what I'm saying is preposterous. Yet I am certain. I'm quite angry, you know. So much so that I feel myself bursting with a desire for retaliation. Since you're wrecking my playthings, how about I break a couple of yours?"

"Should I take that as a declaration of war?"

"Oh, come now, you're the one who struck first."

Mina and I glared at each other silently.

Neither of us showed a hint of killing intent in our eyes. That was what worried me.

Demonstrating aggression gave your opponent information, including your goal, timing, moves, and more. People who were used to killing only revealed their intent to do so when they needed to intimidate another.

Thus, if one accustomed to violence displayed absolutely no killing intent in this kind of situation, I took it as an omen that they were about to act.

"Ha-ha, I'm joking, dear. I quite liked that plaything, but you are *much* more interesting. It would be foolish to lose you over something like this," Mina remarked, relieving the tension by shrugging.

Still, I couldn't let my guard down. She could start a fight at any moment.

With that in mind, I decided to probe for information. "Once again, I did not kill him. But even if we suppose I did, you acted first. I told you not to lay a hand on my friends."

"Oh my, you found out about that? He's my current favorite. He's such a nice boy, so innocent, funny, and clumsy. That was why I scooped him up. Ah, but that puts me in a real pinch. I admit I did reach out to one of your friends, which means I don't have the right to kill one of your lovers. We'll have to call this one a draw."

My doubt became conviction. Mina was involved in Naoise's disappearance.

"...What did you do with Naoise?"

"You'll understand soon enough. How about we go ahead and drop this tedious talk? I want to move on to why I'm here."

"That wasn't why you wanted to talk to me?"

"Nope. I don't really care about that stuff."

What was this demon doing? I had killed one of her favorite puppets, she'd threatened to do the same to one of the girls, and she was connected to Naoise's recent disappearance. Yet she wasn't interested in any of that?

"The next demon is about to appear. He is extremely strong. You and your adorable attendants won't be able to defeat him alone. Don't worry, though. You're going to receive reinforcements."

"Reinforcements? You're not going to help us, are you? I thought you didn't want the other demons to find out you're opposing them?"

"Heavens, no. I'm looking forward to this. I'm sure you've already reasoned out what I mean."

"I don't know what you're talking about."

That was a lie. Judging from our conversation, I could guess what Mina was alluding to.

"I compiled some information on the demon. Have a look at these papers. Ah, but don't read them here. I've given you all the knowledge I can share, and I don't feel like telling you anything else. Your way with words might cause me to let something slip."

At that, Mina took her leave. Left alone, I read over the files she'd left.

I could never have imagined that something like this would happen right after my date.

The appearance of a new demon was concerning, but we weren't going in blind this time, so I was confident we could handle it.

Chapter 19 | The Assassin Shares His Plan

According to Mina's intel, the next demon was going to appear near a city called Jombull in northern Alvan. Given its location on the border, it was a hub for international trade, with much commerce conducted with Dia's homeland, the Soigelian Kingdom. It wasn't the economic powerhouse the harbor town of Milteu was, but it was relatively prosperous.

The demon was expected to show up very soon—in a mere three days.

Jombull was only about eight kilometers from Tuatha Dé, so a disaster there would undoubtedly affect my home as well. After researching Jombull's population, I discovered it was just short of the number of lives required to form a Fruit of Life, even if the demon sacrificed every person in the city. That meant it would probably attack Tuatha Dé next.

"So the demon's going to strike Jombull? I've been there before. It's a nice city," said Dia.

"It is. And as a Tuatha Dé, I can't afford to let it fall," I replied.

Jombull was an important trading partner for our domain. It was always our first option when we needed to purchase any goods, and it was a place to sell the things we produced.

There were plenty of other towns that could fill that role, but they were all too far.

"Did you find this using your usual information network?" Dia asked as a bump on the road jostled us in our seats in the carriage.

"That's right," I answered.

I was hiding Mina's true identity, so I told Dia that I had procured the data on the demon.

Two other people were accompanying Dia and me. One of them was Tarte. She was carefully reading the files I had put together on the demon. I'd added knowledge obtained from the Alam Karla to what Mina initially gave me, performed analysis, and written out a strategy.

"I can't believe you really came," I admitted to the last person traveling with me.

"Of course I did," answered a purple-haired girl possessed of unrivaled beauty. People always claimed that purple was the color of nobility, and seeing Nevan convinced me that they were right.

I'd promised to take her along when we fought demons.

"You're placing an awful lot of trust in my words," I remarked.

House Romalung had its own information network, yet they had not been aware of the impending appearance of a new demon.

I'd only obtained the information because I had a demonic informant of sorts.

"I am truly amazed you found something that House Romalung hasn't even gotten a whiff of," Nevan said with a giggle.

"Aren't you curious how I discovered it?"

"From your usual intelligence network, surely?"

"That's right."

Nevan's friendly grin never left her face. She wasn't asking me where I got the information because she knew doing so would be pointless. That didn't mean she had given up. She had made a clear declaration of intent to find out for herself.

Tarte's head looked about ready to steam as the carriage trundled along. "Urgh, this demon is too strong. It's not fair!" she complained as her eyes scanned over the documents repeatedly in evident frustration.

It was funny how she made even that kind of behavior look adorable.

"You're right about that. The next demon is the Beast King Liogel. As you might expect from his name, he shares several qualities with large cats," I explained.

"Lions are so strong," commented Tarte.

"Yeah. Their feline muscles give them flexibility, leaping ability, and explosive athleticism. Their reflexes are also impressive, and like all carnivores, they are capable of tremendous concentration. We can use that last characteristic to our advantage, however," I expounded.

If Liogel indeed was a solo-type demon, I believed he would be easy to assassinate.

"Why would strong concentration make the demon easier to kill?" inquired Tarte.

"A carnivore's focus becomes very narrow when hunting prey. I become the same way when sniping—I shut off all else except for me and my target. That depth of concentration is why I don't miss," I responded.

"Oh, I understand. Its focus means more blind spots, and it will be slow to respond to any attacks that come from them," Dia reasoned.

"That's exactly right. It's why I always need an assistant when sniping. With Tarte present as my attendant, I can give a target my undivided attention."

You make yourself more vulnerable when stalking prey. That was an unavoidable fact.

Herbivores possessed a wide field of vision and never dropped their guard, which gave them a better chance of escape.

Hunters, however, were different. They only needed to concentrate when they intended to kill. They devoted everything to that one moment and easily surpassed their opponent's level of concentration. As a trade-off, their attention didn't last long, and their vision was significantly narrowed.

"But you still think the fight will be difficult, right, Lugh?" questioned Dia.

"That predator nature would be a weakness if Liogel were alone, but he has a harem, as is typical of lions."

Lions formed groups of females centered around one male. The Beast King Liogel was not the kind of demon that could produce monsters, but a pack always accompanied him.

"Um, what do you mean by 'harem'?" asked Tarte.

It was Dia who replied. "I'll answer that one. Let's see... Take Lugh, me, and though I haven't met her, Maha. You can call our relationship a harem."

"Hold on a moment. Would you mind adding me to that?" Nevan requested, staring at Dia coldly.

"The duke wouldn't like you associating with me. If you get too close to Lugh, Tarte and I will want nothing more than to drive you away," Dia threatened.

"That is not the case. We have a high opinion of you, Claudia. I'm sure any children you bear would be worthy of joining House Romalung. We have firm plans to obtain you. If Lugh ever falls out of love with you, please come to us. We'll prepare seed befitting your brilliance," Nevan stated matter-of-factly.

She was spouting her usual nonsense. Even in matters of possessiveness and love, she was a Romalung above all else.

"Geez, I guess you really are a Romalung daughter. I have no desire to give my children to your house, and what I decide to do if ever Lugh happens to dump me is none of your business. Why do you only want me? What about Tarte?" asked Dia.

"We have no need of her. She's nothing more than an average person who works hard," Nevan said dismissively.

"...Ah-ha-ha," Tarte laughed nervously.

Dia's face twisted in a scowl. "That was a rude thing to say."

"I simply spoke the truth," Nevan shot back.

"U-um, please don't fight over me," Tarte pleaded.

Tarte didn't try to deny Nevan's words...and neither did I. I knew that Nevan's claim was correct, to an extent.

Tarte was not a genius—her intelligence was as average as they came. She was just endlessly sincere and gave everything her best effort. Her sincerity allowed her to digest what she was taught without any prejudice, and her work ethic meant she practiced longer and more intensely than others.

She was a different variety of person compared to me, Dia, and Nevan. However, in my opinion, her genuineness and tireless perseverance were real talents.

"Let's get back on topic. Perhaps I shouldn't have used the word *harem*. It's essentially a pack under the demon's command. The females are pretty close in strength to the male. They possess their own will and are smart and precise. A small, organized group can achieve far more than their numbers would first suggest," I explained.

Liogel's group coordinated, amplified their strengths, and eliminated their weaknesses. A good pack increased the power of each individual many times over.

"Lugh, I'm a little scared of the answer to this question, but are the females monsters? We'll be able to kill them normally, right?" Dia inquired, looking for confirmation.

"Yeah, they're monsters. But apparently, they gain the same properties as demons if the male touches them. Once he dies, they'll resurrect unless slain directly by the hero or within the Demonkiller field."

Dia and Tarte went silent. It was clear they understood how difficult our opponent was.

Finally, Tarte spoke up. "Um, how do you plan on stopping them, my lord?"

"Well, we can't do anything until we separate Liogel from the females. That will be our first goal."

"Do you have a specific method in mind?" questioned Dia.

I nodded. "Yes. You know the weapon I use for Cannon Strike?"

"Yeah, that giant death machine."

"I tinkered with it a bit and made it into a kind of catapult, er, launchpad. With it, I can blast Liogel kilometers away. We'll then take out as many females as we can, making sure to incinerate them so that the demon has nothing of their bodies left to revive. Then we'll just repeat that process."

It sounded like an excessive strategy, but I trusted its efficacy. Plus, I had a backup plan in case the catapult didn't work out.

"You make it sound simple, but I think this is going to be really hard," said Tarte doubtfully.

"I'll make it work. Trust me."

That wasn't a boast. I had a clear vision for this fight. Suddenly, I felt someone's eyes on me. Nevan had been looking at me silently for a while.

"Do you have something to say?" I prompted.

"I just thought it odd that you have a simpler method, yet you're electing not to use it," she answered.

Nevan's words came as no surprise. I did have a method that could end the battle much easier and with less risk, as long as I was willing to make a certain concession.

"Mind if I ask what you're talking about?" I questioned.

"At the academy, you used wide-range and incredibly strong magic to blow up an entire force of orcs in one go. You could just use that again. The females can't revive unless the male touches them, right? That magic of yours wouldn't leave so much as a scrap behind. Even if some part remained, it'd be blasted too far away. Liogel would revive, but you could take his pack out of the picture in one strike." Nevan was referencing Gungnir and Cannon Volley.

Tarte and Dia looked at Nevan in wonder at her claim that there was such a method.

"I had considered that. The problem is the demon and his monsters could appear near Jombull at any time. The settlement's walls are considerably weaker than those at the academy or the royal capital. If I use spells like that too close to the walls, I'll end up leveling Jombull," I responded.

That was our biggest obstacle. In the battle with the orc demon, the monsters I'd wiped out were far from our forces, and a sturdy barricade protected the academy. When we encountered the beetle demon, the local populace had already been massacred. Things were different this time, however.

"Why is that a problem? It's a battle to save the world. You are the Holy Knight, and the world needs your continued protection. I don't think the people of Jombull are worth putting yourself at risk," argued Nevan.

"We disagree there. If I have to put myself at risk for the chance of saving a thousand lives, I'll do it every time. Don't get the wrong idea, though. If pressed to the point where there is no other choice, I am prepared to sacrifice Jombull. I just don't think that's worth it yet. I believe we can handle a different tactic."

I wasn't going to refute what Nevan was trying to say. I didn't intend to claim that human life was more precious than anything else.

If I died, the world was doomed. Even so, this was a risk I was willing to take.

"Well, as long as you understand the implications." Nevan paused and turned to Dia and Tarte. "What do you two ladies think?"

"I agree with Lugh. He never decides on a route he can't complete," Dia replied.

"Yes, I also believe in Lord Lugh!" added Tarte.

"My, what wonderful trust they have in you," Nevan remarked, her smile slightly different than before. She then clapped her hands as if coming to a sudden realization. "Ah, what made me ask such a foolish question? You had already made up your mind on the number of necessary sacrifices and built your strategy with that in mind, yes? You would never have been so naive. Hee-hee, I'm falling for you all over again. I'll do whatever you need of me. My light magic will give us a better chance of success, but I expect you've been counting on that from the beginning."

Nodding, I praised her. "You understand my tactics well. I took all of that into account when assessing the risk."

"I've never met a man able to see things the way I can. I knew you were the one for me."

The carriage raced toward the site of the decisive battle.

She saw through the part I wasn't intending on mentioning until the end.

I was hiding something from Tarte and Dia. My plan for this battle already assumed a certain amount of damage to the city.

If I truly wanted to minimize lives lost, we would have had to evacuate Jombull. However, doing so would have required exposing my informant to the kingdom, and if people fled from Jombull, there was a high chance the demon would abandon his target. Not knowing where Liogel might strike would result in exponentially greater damage.

My new life may have taught me compassion, but I was still an assassin. I was willing to play the numbers game with human lives.

I couldn't risk the demon altering his course, so I accepted that some people would die due to our fight in Jombull. By my estimation, however, we would save most of the denizens.

Now that I had made that decision, I resolved only to allow a certain number of casualties, and I was determined not to let that integer climb any higher.

Chapter 20 | The Assassin Takes Consideration

We secured lodgings in Jombull upon arrival, electing to prepare in town until the demon attacked. That way, we'd be ready whenever Liogel appeared.

We were holding a strategy meeting as we ate.

"Mmm, the food in this city is so good. This is so nostalgic," Dia said, taking a bite with a look of satisfaction on her face.

We were eating meunière prepared with river fish that had been sautéed in butter. The stir-fried onions helped set the dish apart from similar ones.

The flavor was nothing special, but it must have reminded Dia of home. This city was close to the border with the Soigelian Kingdom, and its influence could be seen even in the food.

"Um, Lady Nevan, is it okay for you to be eating with us?" asked Tarte timidly.

"Of course. As I said the other day, when I travel with you to fight demons, I am a teammate and of the same station as the rest of you," the daughter of House Romalung answered.

I gave one condition for Nevan while traveling with us: She had to agree to simply being a comrade rather than the scion of a duke.

The requirement hadn't been born of a desire to be friendly with her. Rather, maintaining the chain of command was an essential part of operating as a team. Even in a tiny squad like this, the presence of two leaders would dramatically hamper the quality of our performance.

"That doesn't change the fact that you are a high-ranking noble, Lady Nevan…"

"Modesty is certainly one of your best qualities, Tarte, but it's also a weakness. This is how armed forces operate. Even children of elite aristocrats need to follow orders absolutely, and they can't receive any special treatment. If some troops were treated differently than others, everyone would die," Dia explained.

"Dia's correct. I brought Nevan along because she said she could handle it," I added.

"And I can. So, Tarte, please follow Dia's example and just call me by my name," Nevan insisted.

"O-okay, N-Nevan," Tarte stammered, nervously dropping the honorific.

"There you go, that's it. Ah, can you pass the salt, Nevan?" Dia requested.

"Yes, here you are."

Somehow, I felt like dropping the respectful title had been *too* easy for Dia. She was probably used to dealing with eminent nobles.

"You remember my other condition, right?" I questioned.

"Yes, of course. I am not to tell anyone of the information I learn here or misappropriate any of your technology," Nevan answered.

"That's right. We possess technology and tactics that we don't want anyone to know about. When fighting a demon, we can't afford to keep any of our cards hidden. If you can't accept that condition, I will do everything in my power to prevent you from tagging along."

That was another thing we had agreed on beforehand. Nevan was sworn never to reveal the secrets of Gun Strike, Gungnir, Railgun, or any of my other techniques.

It was impossible for me to kill a demon without the powerful spells I'd developed. Furthermore, once I had decided on a plan that used them, I couldn't begin the mission without all my teammates understanding how they worked.

"I will keep my promise. If I decided not to keep it, what would you do?"

"Nothing. It would confirm that you are an enemy whom I can never trust again. You can poke as many holes in this agreement as you like. For example, you could have a lifelong servant of House Romalung tag along and have them share what you saw for you. I am intentionally choosing not to obstruct that kind of loophole. However, know that I will regard you as an enemy if you do so," I cautioned.

"Oh goodness, that would break my heart. Still, are you sure you're willing to treat House Romalung as hostile?"

"Yes. You've made it plain how highly you think of my abilities... And killing you wouldn't be a problem. Even if you are a Romalung."

I intentionally revealed my killing intent to Nevan. That served as a threat and as a show of my determination. Her eyes went wide, and she held her hands to stop them from shaking.

"Ha-ha-ha, you're definitely an assassin. What a cold gaze. But I like that. Please trust me. I won't do anything to displease you. You're my important future husband."

"I don't remember ever consenting to that last part."

"What does your consent have to do with it?"

She really was a Romalung.

"Now that we've cleared that up, let's finish our meal. Afterward, we'll discuss strategy," I announced.

"Yes, let's enjoy the food of the common folk," said Nevan.

"This is a feast," Tarte corrected, looking at Nevan strangely.

The two of them had polar opposite origins. Nevan was born a duke's daughter, and Tarte, in a poor agricultural village.

It was time to put everything aside and eat. I needed to recover from the exhaustion of the long trip.

The next day, we walked through the town to get the lay of the land. I had a map of the city, but I needed to see it with my own eyes.

I had a feeling this battle could turn into urban warfare. That was more likely than not.

The demon had feline characteristics, and he was going to appear right outside the town with a pack of monsters. Liogel was swift and could leap incredible distances. He would reach the city in an instant and jump the walls in one bound. Some of House Romalung's elite soldiers were keeping watch in every direction, but there was no way to keep the demon out.

Yesterday, I'd claimed I couldn't use Gungnir because of the fragility of Jombull's defenses, but that assumed we were lucky enough to intercept the demon outside the city limits. If I used it within the settlement, it would annihilate everything.

"It seems like we won't be able to limit damage to the city no matter where we fight," Tarte lamented, looking around restlessly.

"Jombull is very prosperous. There's nothing we can do to prevent casualties. We aren't gods," I responded.

"I know that, but it's still sad."

I patted Tarte on the head. "You're so compassionate."

Despite her apparent embarrassment, she leaned happily into my gesture. "That's not true. I just don't like the thought of people dying."

"I have a suggestion. Since we are surveying the city's layout, we may as well look for places that could be used to our advantage," Nevan proposed.

"The best way to do that might be to set traps. That could definitely be effective," I responded.

We knew the demon and his monsters were coming ahead of time, so it only made sense for us to prepare for their arrival. Given that we were going up against a demon, however, anything we prepared would need a massive amount of firepower. A trap with that amount of strength would blow up dozens of houses upon activation, and we would need to set multiple of them.

That was another strategy that necessitated sacrifices. However, there were going to be casualties regardless. Thus, I thought it best to lure the demon's pack toward where we set the traps, then use them to keep our enemy confined within a smaller battlefield. That might help contain deaths.

"Then let's do it," urged Nevan.

"There are many places I want to put them, but it'll be difficult. I can handle gathering the materials to make the traps, but placing the things is the issue. People will notice them before the demon arrives," I said.

"You don't have to worry about that. Let's put the traps inside homes. I'll throw money in the residents' faces to buy their houses, so we can prepare as many as we want."

No one would mess with the devices if they were inside purchased homes, so concealing them would be easy.

"Are you okay with that? It's going to cost a lot of money," I warned.

"Using money when you need it is what gives it value," Nevan answered.

"Then I'll take you up on that."

If it increased our chances of success even a little, I was fine with relying on Nevan's assistance.

Ultimately, we purchased sixteen houses and prepared a trap in each one. I made them so they could be activated remotely.

"That was a ridiculous display of wealth," I said to Nevan.

Smirking, she replied, "I make a lot of money."

Once the demon appeared, we were going to engage him outside Jombull for as long as possible. As such, there was a chance the battle might not even make it to the city. Still, that didn't stop Nevan from buying the domiciles at nearly double their market value. Technically, there was still a chance, albeit a slim one, that Liogel wouldn't even show.

I decided to apologize in advance. "Sorry if that turns out to be a waste of money."

"Don't worry about it. Do you think I didn't notice what you were doing? All the buildings you purchased were on sites that would be easy to reuse or conduct business from. Even having bought them at near double the market value, you or I could easily recover the expense for each piece of land," Nevan responded.

"I'm impressed you picked up on that. I looked for structures in good positions for the traps while also ensuring they'd enable us to recoup our investment. I didn't want you to lose money over this," I explained.

Whether Nevan thought it was or not, acquiring all those buildings was a large expenditure. As such, I wanted to think about what would become of our new properties.

"But that wasn't all, was it? You really think of everything... If the area around each of the houses was to get flattened during the battle, the value of each spot would increase many times over. You would make quite a land shark," commented Nevan.

"Wow, you come up with the nastiest ideas, Lugh. I can't believe you bought those places predicting the battle would turn them into vacant land," added Dia.

"I didn't do that part for Nevan. I did it so I would be able to support the people who live in those areas in the case that we bring the battle to those sites." Nevan and Dia tilted their heads in confusion, so I clarified. "If the value of the land goes up, I'll buy it from them at a high price."

"Oh, I understand. Those who lose their domiciles in this battle won't struggle for money or a place to live if you buy their land from them!" exclaimed Tarte.

I nodded. No matter where we brought the fight, there would be a lot of sacrifices. Thus, I chose land that would rise in value if destroyed by the battle to give any displaced the funds to start over.

"Ah, that's what you were doing. You care way too much for other people, Lugh. All that stress is going to make you go bald," Dia stated.

"I don't like the sound of that." I gave a strained laugh. What I was doing was the ultimate hypocrisy, but it was in line with the guiding principles I'd established for myself after being reborn as Lugh Tuatha Dé.

I had no intention of dying, and I wouldn't do anything that might lower the success of the assassination. However, I wished to do all I could to aid the citizens of Jombull within those constraints. This was the kind of thing I would never have considered before my reincarnation.

I finished setting the trap in the final house.

"…That's the last one. Now, all we have left to do is prepare. Nevan, there's something I need to tell you. Naoise will probably show up when we're fighting the demon. He has given up his humanity to obtain power. Such behavior is inexcusable for a noble of Alvan."

During the duel, Naoise had made his thirst for strength apparent, and Mina had promptly scooped him up as a plaything. She'd also told me that the demon would be too strong for me, and someone would arrive to provide help.

All of it led me to believe that Naoise would be making an appearance.

"Wow, that's another piece of information I knew nothing about. I've been so worried about that idiot friend of mine."

"What will you do if that idiot friend becomes our enemy? I'm ready to kill him if necessary."

"So you're saying you will spare his life if possible."

"Do you always have to twist my words around?"

"I also want to avoid killing him if possible… That boy used to be so cute. Calling out 'big sis, big sis' all the time and chasing me around like a puppy. Where did he go wrong?" Nevan smiled. A hint of loneliness showed on her face. She cared about Naoise in a sibling sort of way.

That was something I hadn't expected. Nevan seemed to only ever think of House Romalung's future, and Naoise had nothing to offer her family.

"Anyway, we're done here. The demon could appear at any moment, so make sure you're ready for battle," I instructed.

"Yes, my lord. I'll eat and get lots of sleep!" responded Tarte.

"I'll perform one last check on a new spell I created for this battle," Dia announced.

Pondering for a moment, Nevan said, "Then I will think about how to handle the aftermath."

We had done everything we could. Now it all depended on our performance in the battle.

Chapter 21 | The Assassin Takes Up Arms

Every moment we spent waiting for Liogel, we used to get ready in some fashion. The sun had begun to set, painting the city in evening colors.

It was now the day after Mina told me the demon would appear. There was a chance he wouldn't turn up at all. That was no excuse to let my guard down, however. Her report might have been a little off.

Dia yawned as she performed maintenance on her pistol in our room at the inn.

"You don't look tense at all," I pointed out.

"I can't help it. I kept myself ready all day yesterday," she answered.

"It's too early to assume the demon won't show. You need to remain alert."

"Sorry, you're right. I'll stay focused." Dia slapped her cheeks with both hands.

Tarte, who had also been inspecting her pistol, pinched her cheeks. Unlike Dia, Tarte was too tense and had been wearing herself out.

"...That's strange," Nevan muttered absentmindedly.

"Did something happen?" I asked.

"I didn't receive the regular report from the west."

"Then we should head there."

"This doesn't necessarily mean it's the demon. Whenever a regular report isn't delivered, soldiers positioned elsewhere go to see what happened. It would be best to wait a little longer," Nevan advised.

"You've entrusted the lookout to House Romalung's elite, right? There is no way they would shirk a regular report for some minor trouble. This is worth inspecting ourselves," I argued. Then I attached my Leather Crane Bag to my waist. I was already fully equipped otherwise.

Tarte and Dia, having finished their maintenance, equipped their respective pistols and nodded.

"You're right, Sir Lugh. I was being overly complacent," Nevan confessed.

"It might be nothing, but it's worth knowing for certain," I said.

The four of us dashed quickly out of the inn.

"Looks like I was right," I muttered as we headed west.

I didn't even need to cross past the city wall to be sure that the demon had killed the Romalung soldiers. Before our very eyes, a gruesome scene was unfolding.

The Beast King's pack was slaughtering citizens.

The monsters all lacked manes, making them resemble lionesses. That meant they were the demon's underlings. The demon himself was not present.

We couldn't take the monsters lightly, however. Their fangs

crunched through human skulls as if they were made of sand, and their claws tore through flesh like butter. The people cried and screamed as they ran to escape.

The monsters stood about two meters tall and three meters long, twice the size of an average big cat.

I probed the surrounding area using wind magic and discovered that the monsters were spread around the city. That they were so scattered was a problem.

As I was pondering the best course of action, I saw a lioness monster appear behind a woman fleeing with a child in her arms.

"H-HEEEEEELP!" she screamed.

The creature's claws threatened to rake her at any moment.

"Gun Strike!"

I chose Gun Strike instead of Cannon Strike for precision accuracy to keep from hitting innocents.

True to my aim, the tungsten bullet struck the lioness square in the forehead. The bullet made a hard sound on impact, however, and was repelled.

The lioness lost interest in the mother and child and leveled its glare at me.

"Go, quickly!" I yelled.

"O-okay!" the mother responded.

Fortunately, I had managed to save the two, and I'd learned something about the enemy in the process.

"Guess this means their fur is stronger than steel," I remarked.

That was the only explanation for my shot bouncing off. There was one more thing troubling me, too.

Gun Strike could easily puncture objects with the hardness of an iron plate, and even if the enemy's defenses were too sturdy to penetrate, the immense force of impact should still inflict damage.

Yet the bullet hadn't stopped upon collision with the lioness's head. It had slid off its fur.

The creature's hair had to possess the toughness of steel while still being flexible. Perhaps the natural oils and fats coating the fibers made them slippery.

If my supposition was correct, then bullets wouldn't accomplish much, and neither would slashing or blunt attacks. This was going to make these monsters very difficult to deal with.

"It's coming!" I shouted in warning.

My Gun Strike may not have wounded the lioness, but it had succeeded in garnering its ire. The monster charged at me by itself.

"ROOOOOOOAR!"

The lioness moved at a breakneck pace, racing forward at top speed after the first step. It was easily moving at 300 kilometers per hour, and I was 40 meters away. It would reach me in about half a second.

That wasn't enough time to perform the incantation for Gun Strike. The creature's fur would render that effort worthless anyhow.

I understood now how these monsters had been able to massacre House Romalung's elite soldiers. Not even they could do anything about this ridiculous armor and swiftness.

Unfortunately for the lioness, it was underestimating me. Its approach was far too linear.

I drew a pistol I kept concealed in a pocket inside my jacket. It was a mechanism too complex to be fabricated via magic, so I needed to carry it around.

However, having it on my person meant I could use it without casting a spell, giving me a source of rapid-fire projectiles with superior force and precision.

I like how this came out. It feels good in my hands.

I only had half a second before the lioness pounced, but that was more than enough time to draw the gun and loose several rounds. I had practiced this motion thousands of times in my previous life.

Swiftly aiming the weapon, I shot twice in quick succession.

While this firearm's force was superior to Gun Strike, it was impossible for a gun the size of a pistol to achieve the power necessary to penetrate that hard and slippery fur. Yet I still had a way to slay the monster.

Since the fur was impenetrable, I merely had to aim for a spot without any. There was one such weak point that nearly all animals shared—the eyes.

My bullet tore through one of the lioness's eyes, shredding its soft vital organs and killing it immediately.

That didn't halt the momentum of the monster's charging, however. I stopped the creature by kicking it in the head with one of my boots, the bottom of which was fitted with metal.

Doing so turned out to be the right choice. Had I used my hands, they would've been skewered by the needlelike hairs.

"Lure the scattered monsters and focus on thinning their numbers here as much as you can!" I commanded.

The demon Liogel had spread his pack throughout the city to slaughter as many as possible. That decision would keep him from reaching all of the monsters and reviving them with his touch. We needed to take out as many of the creatures as we could now.

"Sounds good," Dia said with a nod before burning the corpse

of the lioness I'd killed. Reducing the bodies to ash was our way of keeping Liogel from restoring them.

A new lioness monster was already drawing near. As if it had sensed the death of a pack member, possibly from the smell, it paused its slaughtering of townsfolk and eyed me with clear hatred. At its roar, two more of its kind rallied to it.

Even when driven by intense emotion, these creatures were calm and intelligent... Their leader must have been thorough with their training.

"They're coming!"

The lionesses seemed to decide that three was enough, then spread out and dashed forward. One of them raced at me in a zigzag pattern to keep me from training my gun on it, while the other two targeted Tarte and Dia, respectively.

The quick and complex movement of the lioness made it impossible to hit at all, let alone aim precisely for its eyes. That said, I had plenty of other cards up my sleeve.

The zigzagging may have taken shooting it out of the question, but it also meant the monster would take longer to reach me, which gave me time for an incantation.

I finished my spell when the monster was a step away from me.

"Wind Cage!"

This was an original bit of magic that Dia and I had created. It formed a space in front of the caster a few meters wide and filled it with carbon dioxide. Any living creature that stepped into the area would immediately have the oxygen sucked out of its lungs, suffer massive brain damage, and then fall into a coma and die.

No matter how hard this lioness's fur was, it was a living creature. There was no escape.

Wind Cage was one of my favorites and very easy to use. With my opponent taken care of, I checked to see how the other two were doing.

I grinned upon realizing how reliable they both had become.

"*Wind Bullet!* I did it, my lord!"

Tarte filled her Tuatha Dé eyes with mana and dodged the claws of the attacking lioness by a hair. No sooner had she done so than she immediately launched a ball of compressed air through the lioness's chin from just above the ground.

Because it was made of wind, the projectile ripped into the monster's fur and struck it unconscious. Tarte didn't waste a moment, jumping forward and plunging a dagger through one of the creature's eyes once it was incapacitated.

Tarte was making fantastic strides as an assassin.

Wind Bullet was a spell that Dia had developed and could be invoked with a very short recitation. However, while the incantation time was brief, it was still impossible to strengthen your body with mana as you chanted. Reducing yourself to your raw physical strength and rendering yourself momentarily defenseless to counter with magic took incredible concentration and bravery.

Dia dispatched her foe utilizing a simpler method.

"*Firestream!* ...You're not escaping that."

Our burning the first lioness had taught us that the monsters were vulnerable to heat. With that in mind, Dia used her powerful mana to form a torrent of flame that gave the beast no room for escape.

Such a mighty spell required a decent incantation time. Dia had undoubtedly started speaking it well before the lionesses even charged at us. Her foresight and advanced ability to correct her incantation time to finish at precisely the right moment were what enabled her to catch an enemy moving at such high speed.

I heard clapping. It was coming from Nevan, who had just been standing one stride behind us and observing.

"I knew you were strong, Sir Lugh, but I am floored by how capable your servants are," she said.

"I wouldn't have brought them if they were a burden. They're very valuable assistants and important to me in battle," I answered.

Not too long ago, I may have left Dia and Tarte behind, opting to do this alone. They'd both grown a lot and had reached the point where I felt comfortable letting them watch my back.

"Hee-hee, your relationship is so wonderful. And you, little miss maid. I am amazed you possess such strength, considering your average talent. I suddenly find you very fascinating," commented Nevan.

"Talent is important but not everything. But forget about that. Our real target has finally arrived," I said.

There was a reason we'd made such a show of killing those lionesses. The creatures had spread throughout the city to butcher the citizens. Killing the monsters one by one was inefficient; they were unbelievably swift, and chasing them all down was unrealistic. Trying to catch them would only allow them to kill everyone in the city.

That's why our strategy was to garner our enemies' attention.

If they were as similar to lions as they appeared, then they would notice the smell of their packmates' flesh burning. A pack was a family, so the monsters had to come seeking revenge. In fact, my scheme was already paying off.

I detected something with my probing wind magic. A large group was making for us, at the center of which was a noticeably big presence.

"We're dead if they catch us. Run!"

"Yes, my lord!" obeyed Tarte.

"There's a trap site nearby, right?" confirmed Dia.

That was why I had engaged the monsters here. I'd judged that we would have enough time to reach the traps before they were upon us.

"Nevan, it's time to quit your spectating. I know you can fight, too," I stated sharply.

The daughter of House Romalung seemed a bit disappointed. "Oh goodness, I suppose I have no choice, then. That's unfortunate. I wanted to learn more about you three."

The enemy had already latched on to our scent. They hadn't spotted us yet, but I was sure they would be able to follow us.

Taking on this number of enemies head-on would be tough. That was why I'd set the traps.

Chapter 22 | The Assassin Sets a Trap

We sprinted as the demon raced toward us with incredible speed. Our destination was one of the spots where we'd laid a trap.

"Uh, it's a little late to say this now, but I think it would have been better to continue fighting them individually," Nevan remarked, somehow able to speak normally as we dashed.

"You're not wrong. They were definitely weaker when spread out. However, there are two reasons I disliked that option," I responded.

"Let me hear them."

"First, I hoped to limit damage to the city. We don't know how long it would've taken to go around wiping all the monsters out. Many innocents could've died."

"You're so compassionate."

"I told you earlier. I'm not swayed by emotion, but I prefer to save the lives I can."

I'd elected not to evacuate Jombull beforehand because I was afraid the demon would change its target. Still, I was gathering the monsters together, thereby limiting potential destruction, and I'd also made preparations using Nevan's political influence and my own authority as a Holy Knight so that the populace could be quickly led to safety in case anything went awry.

"What's your second reason?"

"Rounding them up like this will be much quicker and safer than slaying them all individually."

Fighting the lionesses had made me keenly aware of how dangerous they were, as well as the best way to combat them. Dia and Tarte would have been in trouble had the battle dragged on too long.

"I see. I knew I could count on you."

"I'd rather hear you say that *after* we've won."

We turned the corner onto a wide street, though it wasn't quite spacious enough to be dubbed a main thoroughfare. A pack of lions was at our heels.

The demon finally shows himself, I thought. Beast King Liogel was among our pursuers. His presence was so intense that it nearly felt overwhelming.

The females were already big, but he was a size larger. All of the demons I had previously encountered were humanoid, but Liogel was far more animalistic. He possessed a golden mane, and powerful mana burned within him.

Upon close inspection, I spied him gathering natural magic power from the atmosphere.

"They've caught up to us! Should we try to stop them?!" Tarte cried out in panic.

Just as she said, the monsters had closed the gap all but completely, and there were still more of them arriving.

Dia was the slowest on our team, and the rest of us were running at her pace so she could keep up. The monsters would be on us in a mere ten seconds.

"No. This is fine," I stated.

At this rate, our enemies would pounce before we reached the traps, but if we could gain a few seconds with a final spurt, the timing would be perfect.

"Dia, Nevan, proceed as planned. Tarte, carry Nevan on your back," I commanded.

Nodding, Dia responded, "Okay, I'll go ahead and start my incantation."

"My time has finally arrived," Nevan declared.

Dia and Nevan began intoning as they ran. They were both casting powerful spells that required nearly all of their mana, which meant they had to drop their physical strengthening and decelerate.

I picked up Dia while Tarte took Nevan, and we increased our pace from that of a long-distance race to that of a one-hundred-meter dash. Neither of us would last long while supporting another person, but a full sprint should earn us ten extra seconds before the demon and his monsters reached us. That brief amount of time was all we needed to get to the traps and for Dia and Nevan to complete their incantations.

Sure enough, our final push got us there without being caught.

The demon Liogel was behind us with twenty-seven of his underlings in tow. They were aligned precisely the way I wanted, thanks to the spacious street.

The timing and their positioning could not have been more spot-on.

"Dia!"

"Steel Rampart!"

Dia activated the spell that she had been preparing. It was an original one she had created.

An enormous metal wall erupted from the ground.

If it had been shallow, the monsters would have merely leaped over. However, Dia's Steel Rampart was ridiculously big—five meters thick and fifteen meters tall. Its incredible scale was why she needed so much time to execute the spell.

Those lionesses at the front of the pack crashed spectacularly into the barrier. The ones slightly behind them made a snap decision to jump, but they also collided with the wall after failing to scale it.

The creatures descended into mass confusion as they piled up in front of the obstruction.

Even still, we needed to maintain our focus. Our enemies were in disarray now, but once they calmed down, they'd realize they could leap over the houses flanking either side of the street.

We couldn't allow them enough time to notice that.

"Stun Flare!"

Nevan finished her incantation next.

It was a light spell that Dia had crafted after Nevan explained the basics of the element. Dia had finished it just in time, despite only beginning her studies on light magic a few days ago.

Nevan lobbed luminous spheres the size of human heads over the wall, aiming for the traffic jam of monsters.

"Put your backs to the wall and close your eyes!" I shouted.

One second later, a soundless flash bathed the world in a white glow.

Stun Flare was not an attack spell—it was designed for suppression. The magic produced an intense flash.

However, when Nevan, one of the top five greatest mages in the country, released it with her full strength, it did far more than temporarily blind. It burned out the retinas of any who saw the spell, robbing them of sight forever.

It was a surefire way to destroy a target's vision. At the very least, it would sear the eyes of the lions and agitate them further.

Dia stopped the creatures in their tracks with Steel Rampart, and Nevan nailed them in place using Stun Flare. Our preparation was now complete.

"Put on your masks!" I commanded, covering my face with one myself. Then I pressed a switch I had stored inside my jacket.

The houses surrounding the now-immobile lions blew up. They were buildings we had purchased beforehand and were filled with bombs.

Like Stun Flare, the explosives were not intended to kill the monsters. I wasn't foolish enough to think that a blast of that scale was enough to kill a demon and all of his underlings.

They were actually sound and stink bombs.

The explosives released a sound loud enough to shatter all the glass in nearby panes.

The noise could rupture one's eardrums, rock their brain, and utterly destroy their semicircular canals. The stench would knock the strongest of people unconscious in an instant and wreck their olfactory cells.

If we hadn't worn our masks, we would've lost our hearing and sense of smell for the rest of our lives.

I ran to the other side of the rampart immediately after the explosion and started an incantation. No lionesses tried to stop me.

That wasn't a surprise. Stun Flare had blinded them, and the traps had ruptured their eardrums and ruined their noses. With those three senses gone, they were unable to perceive anything.

Because these monsters took after cats, they possessed superior smell and hearing. I'd found a way to turn their overly sensitive noses and ears against them and inflict massive damage.

That had been my goal all along. If I couldn't kill them all, I decided that it was optimal to prioritize rendering them helpless.

Now I could pursue Liogel without fear of interference from his underlings. He was recovering by using his power as a demon, but he still couldn't see me.

I pulled a specially made cannon fitted on a large pedestal from my Leather Crane Bag. The bullet was 720 mm, six times larger than what I used for Cannon Strike. The ends were flat, and a hook was attached to the sizable projectile.

This was what I intended to use to knock the demon far enough away that he wouldn't be able to restore the monsters as we wiped them out. I'd designed the bullet so that it wouldn't penetrate Liogel's body but instead dig into his flesh and send him flying from the force of impact.

The cannon was loaded with Fahr Stones, enabling me to fire it using the mana I had poured into the spell I was chanting.

"Cannon Strike!"

I launched the warhead from its barrel.

Liogel's eyes, ears, and nose were all wrecked like the lionesses', and he had not yet healed. The attack was guaranteed to hit him. At least, I thought so.

Guess I should've expected no less of the Beast King, I mused, impressed.

Although Liogel shouldn't have been able to see, he used his right arm to knock the bullet aside, even as it raced toward him quicker than the speed of sound.

"I CAN SEE YOU!!!"

The projectile blew off Liogel's right arm, but he successfully diverted it while remaining rooted to the spot.

It was an astonishing feat, to be sure. Fortunately, I had a backup plan that I was already working to enact.

I dashed forward immediately after the Cannon Strike, and the moment I finished another incantation, I touched Liogel's body where he couldn't reach now that his arm was gone.

It was time for my ace in the hole…

"God spear, *Gungnir!*"

Going by firepower alone, this was the strongest spell I had. Its major drawback was that it took ten minutes for the spear to come back down. This time, however, I had devised a trick to get around that.

That trick was to skip the spear and just launch my target into the sky instead. I would lift the enemy into the air until just before they reached outer space and then slam them back down to the ground. No living creature could endure something like that. It was a maneuver I'd devised for killing the hero.

Admittedly, using Gungnir this way was not without its own set of drawbacks. I needed a massive amount of mana to use it, so I couldn't devote any to physical strengthening. It still took a long time to cast, too.

What's more, I needed to touch my opponent while only having access to my natural strength during the long incantation process. That didn't seem doable in a fight against the hero. However, if it was an assassination, and she wasn't aware of me, it would be possible for me to reach her.

This was my current best option for killing Epona.

"Enjoy your trip through the skies."

"YOU BRAAAAAAAAAT!" Liogel screamed as he flew up into the air, his body quickly picking up speed. He was going to crash into the ground outside of the city, die, and then surely revive.

I was fine with that. What I wanted was time.

"Tarte, Dia, Nevan. Time to kill the monsters and incinerate the corpses. Then we'll head to where the demon is going to land."

The monsters were now nothing more than powerless lions.

Slaying them all would be a breeze. Liogel would not be able to restore them once they had burned to ash.

I had calculated where the demon was going to land. With his pack out of the picture, we would be able to defeat him.

"Holy cow, you come up with the dirtiest tricks."

"You are as amazing as ever, my lord."

Dia and Tarte emerged from behind the wall and made conversation as they got to work on finishing off the lionesses.

"So this is how an assassin fights. Everything you do is so meticulous and logical. Your preparation was scrupulous; you completely prevented the monsters from exercising their strengths, and now they're helpless. This is wonderful," Nevan praised.

The lionesses were capable as a pack, so I'd prevented them from fighting that way. They possessed superior senses, so I'd overloaded those and destroyed them.

Honest head-on battles were for knights.

"I had sufficient information this time and was able to prepare in advance. Laying a foundation before the kill is key to the assassination," I replied.

Wielding a blade was merely the final touch. An assassin's true strength lay in the process that got them there.

Similarly, wiping out these monsters was only part of the preparation for slaying the real target, Liogel.

So I couldn't let up my guard. Not until Liogel breathed his last breath.

Chapter 23 | The Assassin Challenges the Beast God

The demon's underlings had been managed without issue.

I used wind magic to lift the ferocious stench that had filled the surrounding area into the sky, finally enabling us to take our masks off.

We'd employed weapons of light, sound, and smell. Against such strong opponents, these tactics were far superior to conventional attacks.

"All right, let's gather them up and burn them," I instructed.

Ferocious flames consumed the pile of corpses and thoroughly incinerated them, cinders scattering on the breeze.

"That's one part taken care of. I know I made it myself, but Stun Flare was so much more amazing than I thought it would be," Dia remarked.

"I was surprised as well. I have always been unhappy with light magic's attack power, but I never thought to use it this way. Rendering opponents helpless without killing them is such a brilliant idea! I can think of so many uses for this," said Nevan.

The weakness of light magic was its lack of raw strength. A tremendous amount of light was needed to kill, which demanded a proportionately massive amount of mana.

Light magic was also poorly suited to wide-range attacks,

because the user needed to concentrate the power as much as possible to make up for its poor efficiency.

Stun Flare compensated for light magic's failings by forgoing the usual method of striking at an enemy.

"There's no time for idle chatter. We only have five minutes before he comes back down," I stated.

I understood from the feeling when I blasted him into the sky that the demon weighed over four hundred kilograms.

Gungnir's formula was designed for lifting a mass of one hundred kilograms. I'd created it that way because that was the most I could manage with my instantaneous mana discharge at the time. The amount of magical power I could output had increased since then, but I still couldn't lift the demon as high as I had the spear.

Also, I'd had to perform a quick calculation the moment after discerning Liogel's weight from the feeling of lifting him, making my aim less accurate than usual. Thus, I'd prioritized safety and targeted the middle of an expansive wasteland eighteen kilometers northeast of here.

Even if I was a little off, no damage would come to Jombull.

"We need to hurry, then," responded Dia.

"Yes, he might run away!" agreed Tarte.

"I don't feel like he will. I only caught a glimpse of him, so I'm not sure, but I don't think killing his underlings is enough to frighten him. I think he's the type to be filled with hatred and seek revenge," I explained.

I'd met the demon's eyes for an instant and saw the true nature of the Beast King.

"Whatever the case, we need to make haste. We should seize the first strike," stated Nevan.

"You're right," I answered.

We needed to run... Actually, that wouldn't get us there in time. I elected to use wind magic instead.

"Everyone, grab on to me... Tighter. There, that's good."

"This is really embarrassing," Dia confessed.

Flushed, Tarte asked nervously, "Hwaahhh... Are you sure this is okay, my lord?"

"I wonder how you're going to surprise me next?" Nevan pondered aloud.

Dia was on my right arm, Tarte was on my left, and Nevan was clinging to my back. It would have undoubtedly been a strange sight had there been any onlookers.

As each of the girls threatened to steal my attention with how their bodies pressed against mine, I focused on an incantation. Thankfully, I managed to finish it.

"Ride Wind!"

A gust of air carried us up and propelled us forward. I manipulated the wind further to accelerate.

I was moving slower than usual because I was carrying three people, but we were still gliding at about 120 meters per second, or 430 kilometers per hour. At this rate, we would cover twenty-nine kilometers in just over four minutes.

I could never have maintained this pace running, no matter how much I raised my physical abilities with mana.

"What the heck is this spell?! When did you make this, Lugh?!" Dia screamed.

"When I had a spare moment. It's fun, right?" I answered.

"It is, but that's why I'm upset! I wanted to come up with something like this!"

"Wooow, this is so amazing. We're flying through the air!" exclaimed Tarte.

"This feels so good," Nevan added.

I would have crafted a hang glider using earth magic and manipulated the wind to gain speed in the past. Over time, I'd become capable of skipping that first step and simply riding the air itself.

A physical mechanism was still preferable for long-distance flights, but this was simpler for something quick.

Looking confident, Dia said, "This is going really well. I feel like killing the demon is going to be easy. He's strongest when he's in a pack, right? If we took out his underlings that easily, the head honcho himself should be a piece of cake, too."

"...I'm not so sure about that," I cautioned.

There was one thing I was still apprehensive about. Mina had claimed that Liogel was too powerful for me to beat alone, even admitting she'd prepared someone to aid me for that express purpose.

So far, I hadn't seen anything to make me fear Liogel's strength, and there was no sign of any help arriving. Still, I didn't think she had been lying to me.

I couldn't help but think that Liogel was concealing some hidden ability.

We arrived about five kilometers from the spot where the demon was going to land. We were in the southwest of the wasteland that was located to the northeast of the city.

I had aimed for the center of this region, but because my

calculation wasn't exact, I decided it was best to keep our distance. While monitoring the area with my Tuatha Dé eyes, I kept myself prepared to start running at any moment.

I expected the demon to make impact after twenty more seconds. I wanted to look up, but Gungnir moved so fast that not even Tuatha Dé eyes could perceive it. All I could do was wait for him to land.

Liogel landed three seconds later than I'd expected, and he was around four kilometers south of the spot I'd aimed for and a kilometer from where we were.

It was fortunate that I'd thought to keep some distance.

A *boom* sounded, and dirt was kicked high into the air. A giant crater formed in the ground, and the collision caused a tsunami of mud to rush forward.

I hadn't achieved the same altitude as usual, but the demon's greater mass resulted in about the same power level as a regular Gungnir.

I finished an incantation I had started before he met with the ground and created a metal barrier in front of myself and the girls. It was the same Steel Rampart Dia had used to stop the monsters earlier.

The wave of dirt and rock weakened considerably before it reached us, but it still struck hard against the barricade.

"Let's get moving. He's going to revive soon," I said.

I was sure Liogel had died, given the force of impact, but demons would always revive unless we killed them within the Demonkiller field.

"You're fighting up front this time, Lugh?" asked Dia.

Nodding, I replied, "Yeah. There's something I'm worried about."

If Mina was right about Liogel being stronger than me, Tarte would die if she tried to take him on alone.

Because I would be in the vanguard, I had to entrust the responsibility of smashing the Crimson Heart, the demon's core, to Nevan. I passed her the item she would need for the task.

"I wish you luck," she stated before walking away from us and donning a cloak.

It was a mantle I'd made beforehand. I'd colored it to blend in with the surrounding environs and designed it to mask human odor. It also had high defensive capabilities. The cloak was a gift to help her perform the sniper role.

Dia, Tarte, and I stood at the edge of the crater and peered down at Liogel.

The demon was sitting on the ground and howling.

"GROOOOOOOOOOOOAAAAARRRR!"

Something about the cry sounded mournful. Perhaps he was saddened by the loss of his lionesses.

This was no time to feel sympathetic, however. Liogel was wide open to attack, and I wasn't going to hesitate to take advantage.

I signaled to Dia with my eyes, and she began a chant. Demonkiller's range was short, and if she moved any closer, the demon might notice her before she could hit him. That was why she was preparing Stun Flare to blind him instead. Dia could use it from as far as one hundred sixty meters away.

I began intoning Demonkiller at the same time.

Chapter 23

The plan was to confuse the demon by rendering him sightless, then hit him with Demonkiller.

"Stun Flare!"

Dia had finished her spell. Her working of Stun Flare was even more skillful than Nevan's. Radiant globes sped down toward the demon and expanded.

"GRAAAAAAAAAAAAAWWWWWWWWWW!!!"

Liogel roared just before the glowing spheres burst. Unbelievably, that roar twisted the very air itself, bending the light away.

I wouldn't have been surprised if Liogel had merely defended himself, but he displayed a full understanding of how Stun Flare worked and chose the perfect response. He was more intelligent than I'd first believed.

The demon turned toward me.

"I CANNOT HEAR VOICES OF FEMALES. YOU ALL DO THIS?"

Malice lay heavy in his voice.

My biological instincts were ringing alarm bells, and I subconsciously took a step back.

I'm an assassin. I've trained my mind thoroughly and mastered arts to control my instincts. Yet he's making me feel fear?

"POWER IS RETURNING. EVERYONE IS GONE."

Liogel's body began to swell quickly. His muscles bulged, miasma and mana began to pour out of him, and his mane grew even longer.

What in the world is happening?

I needed to do something. I reflexively drew my gun and opened fire.

Obviously, Liogel would recover from any injury I inflicted.

Even still, I had a feeling this fight could be over for us if he finished this transformation.

All of my bullets hit the mark, but they didn't penetrate Liogel's bulging muscles.

Finally, the demon stood. His back legs had grown to the size of logs, while his torso had shrunk. His front legs sprouted fingers and came to resemble human hands. The claws on his digits thickened and sharpened, each now resembling a black sword.

He looked somewhere between beast and man.

Liogel jumped, displaying speed that put him on par with Epona.

He was aiming to strike me with his right knee, and the attack was too swift for me to evade.

I performed a quick draw and tried to dodge while firing all the remaining bullets in my magazine. The shots bounced off, but the collisions reduced Liogel's speed and allowed me just enough time to get away.

His momentum carried him far past me.

"You're going to pay for this. I'll kill you last. I'll rip off your limbs and make you watch as I defile and eat your women one by one."

The demon had been speaking broken language before, yet now he articulated fluently.

...I see what happened.

The theory that he wasn't too strong himself but was a threat with his pack wasn't wrong, but it wasn't right, either.

Liogel had divided up his strength and shared it with each of the females in his pack, sacrificing his own might in exchange for making the group stronger. Now that the lionesses were dead, the power he'd shared had returned. This was Liogel's true form.

Mina must have known this and hidden it from me.

"Well, this throws a wrench in my plans."

That meant I needed to amend them. I had the ability to cope with any problem, after all.

There was also a chance we could receive an advantageous wild card. Considering Mina's personality, she'd likely withheld information on Liogel's true strength to create the best possible timing to send in her plaything.

Chapter 24 | The Assassin Is Reunited with a Friend

Liogel was even more dangerous than I'd imagined.

Tarte and I nodded to each other, then simultaneously pulled out special syringes and injected a drug into our necks. The chemical only worked for a limited time, but it stimulated the brain and removed its natural limits.

The world slowed down, and my physical capabilities and instantaneous mana discharge increased.

The drug granted me overwhelming strength, but it was a double-edged sword. Humans had limits for a reason, and breaking past them came with serious consequences. The effects of the chemical also only lasted for a short time, and using it continuously led to building a tolerance.

I classified the medicine as a trump card, only to be used in extreme circumstances.

Liogel charged at Tarte instead of me, his mane fluttering in the wind.

Fox ears and a fluffy fox tail sprouted from Tarte's body. This was yet another ace in the hole that only worked for a short while.

We also activated Servant's Devotion. My testing had revealed that it would only work for roughly three minutes.

Tarte understood the situation we were in. She knew that holding back would equal death.

She elected not to dodge, instead charging head-on with her spear. Wind exploded at her back. She used a spell Dia had developed. Its incantation was extremely short, and it loosed a burst of air that launched the user forward.

"Cats are prey for foxes!"

The side effects of Beastification had made Tarte grow belligerent. Servant's Devotion allowed me to hear all of her aggressive thoughts.

Tarte had the look of a carnivore in her eyes. The violent personality that emerged when she used Beastification seemed at odds with her adorable appearance.

The spear in Tarte's hands was different from her usual one. Her typical polearm was divided at the grip with an attachable knife serving as the tip, enabling her to conceal it under her servant clothes. It sacrificed strength and function so she could hide it and keep it on her person.

However, our recent battle with the beetle demon had made me aware that Tarte's weapon lacked raw force. For that reason, I'd made her a new spear that prioritized might over portability.

The spearhead could rotate. A Fahr Stone I'd embedded in the tip caused it to spin rapidly like a drill.

I'd made the point using the toughest alloy I could think of. The result was a magic polearm that cut through diamond.

Utilizing her bolstered strength from the drug, the surge of air at her back, Beastification, and Servant's Devotion, Tarte thrust her weapon at Liogel. The attack had more than just the weight of Tarte's charge behind it. She also used her back and arms to put everything into it.

Tarte's spear was longer than Liogel's claws, so it found purchase first. Liogel would've been able to dodge it had he tried, but he continued forward, likely believing no weapon could pierce his flesh.

That was the wrong move. Tarte's armament was special.

Her spear drilled into the demon's body. However...

"No way. Lord Lugh's lance..."

"You are quite a strong female. It takes skill to cut me."

The tip had gouged into Liogel's chest, but its rotation slowed to a stop just before the demon's heart. His muscle had stopped it.

Liogel then spread his arms wide and swung them both toward Tarte, claws poised to rip her to shreds.

"Not a chance!"

Tarte twisted the handle to use her polearm's hidden mechanism. As soon as she did so, the spearhead rocketed forward with an explosive sound.

The excessive recoil knocked Tarte back about four and a half meters, and the tip of her weapon tore through Liogel, sending him flying. After landing, Tarte affixed a spare spearhead. Liogel was pinned to a boulder three and a half meters from where he'd been a moment before. The spinning tip had a hook that kept it lodged in the demon and affixed him to a boulder.

"This new spear is so useful!" Tarte exclaimed.

Her weapon was both a polearm and a high-caliber gun.

The tip itself was embedded with a Fahr Stone to power the rotating mechanism. It was designed to be used as a rotating spear most of the time, and when necessary, the Fahr Stone could be activated to perform a Cannon Strike.

I'd constructed it in a way I believed suited Tarte's fighting style. She was not an especially skilled marksman. I'd fashioned the armament to fly in the face of what cannons were supposed to be.

Great job, I praised mentally before taking off at a run.

I was not an observer in this fight. My role was to create a sure opening for Dia to strike with Demonkiller.

With Liogel still trapped on the boulder, I sprinted toward him and began chanting. I was using Multi-Chant and the skill I found in its depths called Quick Chant to prepare two spells simultaneously.

Looking annoyed, Liogel gripped the hooked spearhead and ripped it out, tearing his own flesh as he did so, and glared at me.

"ROOOOOOOOOOOOOOOOOOOOOOOOOAR!!"

The demon howled. It wasn't just for intimidation. The sound created a mana-empowered shock wave. It threatened to lift me into the air and blast me away. Fortunately, I entered range to use my spells and finished my incantations just in time.

"Wind Cage! Ice Prison!"

Two spells took effect.

The first was a wind one that filled the area around the target with carbon dioxide to rob their lungs of oxygen. The second was water magic that restrained the enemy by encasing them in thick ice.

My real objective was to entrap Liogel with the latter of the two spells, but he'd never stand still long enough for it to take hold. Thus, I'd had to hold him with Wind Cage first.

Just as I'd intended, the demon fainted immediately after the oxygen was sucked out of his lungs, and ice formed around him.

The frozen water was close to four and a half meters thick. There was no way he would be able to move. This was ice at absolute zero. Such intense cold alone was going to render Liogel immobile. No matter how strong the demon was, it was worthless if he couldn't move.

"*Good job, Lugh. I'll take it from here,*" Dia signaled to me with her eyes as she passed by and headed toward Liogel. Her Demonkiller chant entered its final stage. The spell could permeate ice. It was the perfect chance to hit Liogel.

I started chanting a composite spell using Multi-Chant. I was preparing Railgun.

Nevan was taking care of sniping duties this time and was currently locked on to Liogel, but it wouldn't hurt to have some insurance. The moment Demonkiller made impact, Nevan's shot and my Railgun would pierce the demon's Crimson Heart together.

Dia finished her incantation, all but guaranteeing our victory.

That's when I felt a chill.

I could feel that something was wrong. After canceling my Railgun spell, I grabbed Dia's collar, put her behind me, then threw a Fahr Stone forward and directed the explosion.

"Hey, what the heck was that for?!" she shrieked.

I'd caused her to fall on her back and miss Demonkiller when I yanked her from behind. The Fahr Stone explosion would likely undo all our hard work to trap Liogel in the ice, too.

I'd known the consequences of my actions, however. There was something definitely off about all of this.

There was nothing supernatural about an assassin's hunches. Assassins were constantly probing their surroundings, so they learned to pick up on even the most trivial of signs.

Normally, I would want to investigate those signs to judge the level of danger, form a plan, and decide how to react, but there were many cases where time did not allow for that. In such instances, I had to rely on my vast experience and make snap choices.

That was the sixth sense of an assassin.

"Looks like I was right," I muttered.

The Fahr Stone cracked, and an explosion aimed at the demon scattered fumes and fragments of metal. At the same time, a blast from within the ice sent frozen shards flying in all directions like buckshot.

The two explosions collided, carving traces of destruction into the surrounding environment.

And then...

"Tch..."

I saw Liogel, charging toward me with his body low to the ground. He slashed up with his claws. Although his body was covered in cuts and burns, and chunks of skin and bone were missing, he didn't seem fazed in the slightest.

Even the explosions hadn't deterred the demon. Liogel passed directly through them, racing straight for me. Running into those blasts was a reckless and suicidal move, and that was precisely why it caught me by surprise.

The explosions, the light, and the dust obstructed my senses almost entirely, rendering me unable to rely on my assassin's sixth sense.

This was bad. I had no chance of dodging against Liogel's swiftness. The best I could do was evade a lethal wound.

Before the blow was struck, a shaft of light pierced the demon's limb at the elbow, sending his forearm flying.

The remaining half of Liogel's right arm passed centimeters

Chapter 24

in front of my face. I immediately countered by throwing a Fahr Stone into his mouth and used my feet not to kick him, but to push off of him and gain some distance.

The Fahr Stone erupted in the demon's maw, blowing off his head and neck.

While keeping an eye on him, I moved away and assumed a formation with Dia and Tarte.

"Nevan saved me."

She was the one who had come to my rescue. That attack had likely been what she'd been readying to launch after Dia's Demonkiller pierced Liogel's heart.

I would've been seriously wounded if not for her.

"That's amazing she was able to hit from so far away. I'm glad everyone is safe, but this isn't good. The drug and Beastification are going to run out soon. He is too strong," said Tarte.

"You're right about that," agreed Dia.

Tarte was correct. Liogel's power was insurmountable.

I never thought that he would use mana and miasma to free himself, to say nothing of his absurd physical might and defense.

We had used all of our resources in the hopes of ending things quickly, but we'd only managed to barely come up even.

The demon's head grew back.

I had already come up with a new plan, but if it failed, we were finished. While eyeing Liogel closely, I searched for a moment to strike. However, he did something I wasn't anticipating. He ignored us and broke into a full sprint.

I had to stop him from going that direction, or it would spell disaster.

"*Cannon Strike!*"

I pulled a cannon already loaded with bullets and Fahr Stones out of my Leather Crane Bag and fired, but he dodged it. Liogel was no longer acting arrogantly enough to take hits intentionally.

He was now far ahead of us. Catching up to him or hitting him with an attack would be tough.

Liogel was going after our sniper. The previous attack had alerted him to Nevan's presence, and he'd clearly decided to kill her first.

Nevan began firing at the demon as he drew near. She had no problem striking him because she was using light element attacks, and the bolts of magic cut through his body. Unfortunately, the light attacks were very thin, inflicting only small injuries that healed in mere moments.

In a rare show of panic, Nevan grimaced. She had no means of defeating Liogel, and we possessed no way of reaching her in time.

Unless we did something, the demon was going to eat her.

"Shit!" I clicked my tongue and ran.

This is really bad. I can't help her... No, think. There's no way I'm going to watch a comrade die.

That was when it happened.

A large ebony sword descended from above, striking the ground before Liogel. I expected the demon to ignore it and keep running, given his previously displayed stubbornness, yet he stopped in his tracks.

A man dressed entirely in black landed on the sword's hilt. He crossed his arms, and his cloak fluttered in the wind behind him.

I understood why Liogel halted. A terrible, sinister power was emanating from that blade. It even surpassed Gáe Bolg, a divine treasure I once encountered.

Chapter 24

With no one there to answer my questions, the owner of the sword and Liogel faced each other.

"Who the hell are you? Are you the same as us? You have our scent," the demon snarled.

"The same as you? Ha, so that's how you see me. Truly, I have fallen."

I hadn't been sure of the man's identity, because his clothes obscured his face, but after hearing him speak, there was no mistaking him. The owner of that overwhelmingly mighty sword was someone I knew very well.

I thought he might show up, but the timing couldn't have been better.

Liogel scowled. "Do not interfere. I need to tear off that man's limbs, then defile and eat his women in front of his eyes."

"I won't allow it. Those are my friends, and this girl is special to me."

"Then I'll tear you to shreds like the others."

"You sure talk big for a pawn who is going to demonstrate my greatness. You will serve splendidly. I will prove here and now that I am no longer stuck chasing behind Lugh."

The swordsman in black jumped off the hilt and drew the sword from the ground.

"Now behold the new power I obtained by falling to the darkness, nay, by coming to rule over it. Then engrave my name into your mind. I am Naoise, the Hero of Darkness!"

He declared his name as if he were an actor in a theater getting high off a performance.

The lion and the Hero of Darkness then crossed blades.

"How awful...," I whispered absentmindedly upon witnessing Naoise's transformation.

I was not going to let Mina get away with this. I was horrified by what she had done to my friend.

My hands balled into tight fists.

This was what she'd meant by making Naoise her plaything. I hadn't been able to stop it.

Regrets would have to wait, however. For now, I needed to focus on the task at hand. All that mattered was killing Liogel.

After the battle, I'll do everything I can to treat Naoise. I owe it to him after failing to save him from this.

Chapter 25 | The Assassin Fights with His Friend

Naoise had changed entirely since I last saw him. It wasn't just his clothes that were different; he seemed a wholly other creature.

Miasma was leaking from his body. That meant he had become some manner of monster or demon. Naoise could never go back to the way things were before.

"Did you really desire power so desperately that you were willing to sacrifice your humanity?" I muttered.

There had been signs things were headed in this direction.

From the moment I met Naoise, it was clear that he thought himself to be exceptional. Yet he despaired when faced with the hero's absurd strength. Later, he grew jealous when I, his supposed equal, began racking up accomplishments. He then decided that if he couldn't match my individual strength, he would show his worth by creating an order of knights.

But I had rejected his efforts… And this was the result.

His present state was my fault.

I went to check on Nevan.

"Are you okay?"

"I had a bit of a fright. Still, this hurts my feelings, Sir Lugh.

Don't make that expression… I'm capable enough to buy you time to come save me."

"Sorry, it seems I underestimated you."

Nevan wasn't the kind who overestimated herself or tried to show off. Considering she would likely work with Dia, Tarte, and me again, I didn't want to misjudge her. Doing so could endanger the entire team. Nevan was smart, and she wouldn't pretend to be capable of more than she was.

I decided to hold a training match with her sometime in the future. That would allow me to determine her strength. It was perilous to overestimate her, but the same could be said of underestimating her.

"Naoise has gotten really strong," Nevan remarked as she and I watched him fight. He was taking on Liogel alone and matching the demon blow for blow.

If I tried to join now without understanding Naoise's power, it could put us both at risk. Understanding his abilities first was paramount.

Meanwhile, the others readied themselves to strike at any moment if an opportunity for a lethal blow presented itself. Tarte enveloped her spear with lightning, Dia began chanting Demonkiller, and Nevan prepared a rapid-fire light spell together with the weapon I gave her.

"That blade is incredible," commented Nevan.

"Yeah. It's ominous and powerful. If you told me it wasn't a weapon but a demon in sword form, I might believe it," I agreed.

"That idiot, no, that *imbecile's* swordsmanship looks the same as it ever did, though. First-class but not quite elite. His physical capabilities have improved, but not past human levels. His ability to strengthen himself with mana is still crude, which is a shame.

He can only match that demon because of the tremendous energy flowing into him from the sword. Most astonishingly..." Nevan trailed off.

"All injuries inflicted on the demon with that weapon aren't regenerating. I didn't think that was possible," I finished.

The black greatsword Naoise wielded was tremendously strong. Liogel's claws could easily cut through steel, but the blade parried them without a taking a scratch.

The sword increased its owner's power with miasma. It was also keen enough to cut through Liogel's skin and prevented the demon from healing.

It was possible that Naoise's transformation hadn't made him mightier at all, but rather just allowed him to use that magic weapon.

The sword was clearly stronger than any object had any right to be.

I'd learned how to make weapons imbued with magic power by researching divine treasures. However, I couldn't get an object to house an advanced spell like Demonkiller.

I didn't even know what the power that was endlessly gushing out of the sword was.

"...Well, I get the picture. I'll go back him up. He'll lose unless we help him," I said.

"That he will. That demon is a swift learner. They're evenly matched right now, which means it's only a matter of time until Naoise loses," Nevan stated.

I had to agree. Liogel's intellect made him a formidable combatant.

My drug had already run out, and my instantaneous mana discharge had returned to normal. Even then, I could still fight if I joined my strength with Naoise.

As I moved to join my friend, I looked back at Tarte and Dia and gave them a sign. If this went as I anticipated, I would need their help.

I drew a gun.

Naoise's physical capabilities had been improved, but his skill was the same as before—perhaps even worse, as he was having trouble controlling his newfound abilities.

I could predict his actions many moves ahead.

The firearm I was holding was a rifle I kept stored in my Leather Crane Bag. It was larger than a pistol, enabling it to fire larger-caliber bullets. The significantly greater amount of Fahr Stone powder packed inside would allow it to pierce Liogel's flesh.

I took a breath, then strengthened my Tuatha Dé eyes. By doing so, I could see a split second into the future. I wouldn't be any use in this situation otherwise.

Hitting your target while they were locked in fierce close combat with another was impossible for a normal person.

I wasn't a normal person, however.

I could even do that without the advantage of my Tuatha Dé eyes. In my previous life, I once shot a target through a passing bullet train window while riding in a car traveling one hundred forty kilometers per hour in the opposite direction.

I had a good understanding of Naoise and Liogel's movements and knew what they'd do next. All I had to think about was aim and timing.

"…"

Wordlessly, I fired a bullet that struck Liogel square in the face, blowing his head off just as he was about to counter Naoise's attack.

It was just a simple lead bullet, imbued with none of the power of Naoise's sword, of course. Liogel's head would heal immediately. My shot accomplished nothing on its own.

Yet...

"Thanks for the backup!" called Naoise.

He sliced the now-exposed Liogel with a downward diagonal slash.

If I created openings, Naoise could wound the demon.

Liogel's head regenerated, but the deep laceration in his shoulder remained, and blood poured from it endlessly.

A bleeding demon was a novel sight. I was interested to see if Liogel's movements would falter if he lost enough blood.

"Witness my power!" Naoise cried.

I see. If a demon's regeneration is cut off, it can't ignore the same weaknesses that all other living creatures share.

Liogel was clearly growing sluggish. That he still fought with precision showed that he was an experienced fighter.

Now that we had turned the tables, Naoise was growing overexcited and started taking large swings. Liogel, on the other hand, maintained precise movements and thrust expertly at Naoise's neck.

It was a good attack. Had I not been there, it would have reached Naoise and maybe even given Liogel a chance at victory. However, I'd foreseen the demon's strike ahead of time.

My bullet blew away Liogel's arm from the shoulder down, throwing off his balance.

"HYAAAAAAAAAAHHH!!!"

Naoise swept his sword sideways with an ecstatic battle cry.

Actually, it was less a battle cry and more a scream full of overwhelming fear and embarrassment from the knowledge that he would have been killed if not for my help. That resulted in a crude attack, which let Liogel easily avoid a lethal injury.

"Naoise…"

I had thought his skills hadn't changed, but that wasn't entirely right. He couldn't control his new power, and he was fighting recklessly. He would've been killed twice already if not for my intervention. The normal Naoise would not have lost his cool, and I knew he would've inflicted a mortal wound using the chance I'd just given him.

Liogel jumped back, and Naoise frantically gave chase. He didn't understand that the demon was luring him.

"ROOOOOOOOOOOOOOOOAAAAARRRRRR!"

The injured Liogel roared at Naoise as he charged, sending shock waves his way. Naoise was knocked off his feet, leaving him wide open. Despite that, Liogel left Naoise and, still bleeding, charged straight toward me.

"I just need to kill you!"

Evidently, he had decided that I was more dangerous than Naoise.

His eyes were focused on the barrel of my gun. He was ready to dodge any shots I fired.

It was an intelligent decision, but a foolish one at the same time. With Liogel's elite level of focus, I didn't doubt he could evade projectiles. However, this was a carnivore's concentration, which meant he only saw what he was looking at.

In other words, he is defenseless against anything coming from his blind spots.

Chapter 25

I had anticipated that Liogel might do this.

I took out a hand grenade in my left hand and threw it. Liogel's response was slow because his attention was trained on the gun.

The grenade exploded in midair, producing the same sound the traps had.

Liogel stood upright from shock. His eardrums ruptured, and blood flowed from his ears.

"I have been waiting for this!"

Tarte, who had been slowly approaching so that Liogel wouldn't notice, stabbed the demon in the side with her lightning-enveloped spear. The electric current ravaged his insides, and the shock forced him to come to a full stop.

Liogel had tried to get up after the blast, but now he was immobilized.

"*Demonkiller!* It's about time."

Dia's Demonkiller forced Liogel's Crimson Heart to materialize, shining bright red. She had chanted the extremely difficult spell perfectly.

The demon couldn't move, and his core was vulnerable. That meant there was one thing left to do.

"*Holy Light Amplifier!*"

Nevan's attack was the finishing blow. She used a spell to accumulate and strengthen light mana with a tool I'd made.

It was a simple object made to solve light magic's output problem by storing a large amount of mana beforehand. If you charged it fully, you could achieve plenty of power with light magic.

Nevan's attack pierced the Crimson Heart in the blink of an eye.

I had intended to use Naoise as a decoy from the beginning.

Then I'd forced the demon to go after me and created a chance to strike. I'd communicated as much to Tarte and the others beforehand.

There was a gaping hole in Liogel's heart, and his life began to fade.

"Argh, y-you bastard… If you just hadn't…"

"That's right. I'm the one who killed you."

The demon tried desperately to claw at me, but before he made contact, he turned into particles of light and vanished.

Liogel, you were strong.

One wrong step might have been the end for me. The difference was that I'd been given intel beforehand and had time to formulate a strategy. In an honest fight, my side would have lost outright.

I paid my respects to the demon. Afterward, I heard clapping.

"So this is the true power of a Holy Knight and his attendants. You did well for a lowly human."

It was Naoise. He approached me wearing his usual grin, emanating miasma as he did so. As he got nearer, I realized there was something different about his expression. It seemed he was looking down on us.

"Let's talk. A lot has happened since you disappeared," I said.

"Splendid idea. I have plenty to say to you as well, Lugh," he responded.

Desperately, I searched for the right words to say to my friend who had changed so much.

Words that would allow us to laugh together once again.

Epilogue | The Assassin Sees Off His Friend

Naoise and I faced each other. Now that we had taken out the demon, there was no one to get in our way.

Tarte and Dia watched us from a small distance with worried expressions.

"I can't believe what you've become, Naoise."

Naoise laughed bitterly and looked at me with a hint of irritation.

"What, do you pity me?"

"That's part of it. Do you think you can still live in human society as you are? Anyone capable of noticing will see the miasma covering your body."

Just like there were people who could sense mana, there were those who could detect miasma. The government was also on high alert for miasma. At the very least, Naoise would not be able to live as a noble anymore.

Miasma even left normal humans feeling uneasy, so Naoise wouldn't last long before being ostracized.

"Why should I care about that? That's a trivial thing compared to this power. I'm sure you saw that I have become stronger than any of you."

"You may be. But that holds little meaning."

While wielding the sword, Naoise's fighting strength was probably greater than mine. But what did it amount to?

Were we to fight head-on, I would be at a disadvantage, but that would change the second Naoise didn't have the sword. Even if he had the sword, I would be able to kill him easily as long as I kept my distance, and I could just run if he tried to get close. A surprise attack from a hidden spot was all it would take.

Power was not absolute. From my perspective, it was a minimal reward to give up your humanity for.

"You're just jealous of me. I know you've secretly always looked down on me. You hid your strength at the academy and mocked me whenever I got a big head! I must have seemed ludicrous in your eyes. Now you don't want to admit that I've surpassed you."

"I've never thought that. I respected you, Naoise… But now you look ludicrous to me. You're a pitiful man who is trying to act tough with borrowed power."

"How dare you!"

Naoise grabbed his sword. His demeanor suggested he would kill me if I continued to talk back to him.

"That is what I mean when I say you look absurd. You are too easily provoked. I won't deny that you've gotten stronger, but you relinquished something more important. Open your eyes. What is it that you want to do with this power?"

"…Silence."

"You once asked me to lend you my strength so that we could change this rotten country. Can you change the nation as you are now? A single powerful individual can't accomplish that on his own. Don't tell me you don't understand that. Your former self thought of strength as only one tool of many, and you searched for allies to do what you couldn't. You were able to gather talent because you had the charm to win people over. I saw that as much more valuable than anything you possess now."

"I said *silence!*"

Naoise drew his sword and swung at me. Tarte and Dia rushed to my side. I, however, just stared at him.

"How did you know I was going to stop my sword?" Naoise asked.

"Because I didn't sense any killing intent."

Naoise's attack had halted right in front of my forehead.

"Sorry, I never meant to do that…"

Naoise sheathed his weapon and buried his face in his hands. The miasma dwelling in his body had made him impulsive. Naoise's great dignity would never have allowed him to do such a thing.

I offered my hand to him.

"Come with me. I can't make you human again. But I can at least teach you how to hide your miasma."

The ominous energy flowing from Naoise appeared warped and unstable. It looked like he had no control over it.

I was confident that it could be commanded. Researching Demonkiller had taught me much on miasma. I'd also studied how to conceal miasma by observing Mina.

With my help, Naoise could do the same as the snake demon, and I could create tools to assist him. Even if Naoise would never be human again, I could help him live in society.

"…Why didn't you tell me you could do something like that? Ha-ha-ha, how pathetic. I wanted to get stronger to prove myself superior to you, but the more I talk to you, the more wretched I feel. I'm leaving. There's something I need to do."

"Where are you going?"

"I have no obligation to tell you that, but we will meet again. You've opened my eyes to what I've done. I had stopped thinking about it, and it had even come to feel good to me. You brought me back to reality. But I thank you for that."

Naoise turned his back. When I tried to speak to him again, Nevan walked past me.

"When did you become such a worthless man? You've always been weak and stupid, but you were never a fool."

Naoise looked back at her. He seemed on the verge of tears.

Evidently, Nevan's words reached him far more deeply than mine.

"Is that how you see me? Nevan, I've always... No, never mind."

"It's not too late. Listen to what Sir Lugh has to say. If you reject his hand, you'll have nowhere left to go."

"...That was the one thing I didn't want to hear."

With that, Naoise took his leave.

Even if I attempted to follow after, I couldn't match his speed. Naoise's physical capabilities were on the level of the hero.

Once Naoise was out of sight, Nevan said, "That old friend of mine has graduated from idiot to imbecile. I wish he had at least thanked me before dashing off."

"I'm sure we'll see him again. It looked like he had a lot to think about," I replied.

He would definitely show up again the next time we fought a demon. Perhaps he could even aid us in getting information from Mina.

Nevan nodded. "Yes, I am sure we will."

"I was surprised to see that Naoise likes you that way," I commented.

"I am aware of his feelings. He's been following me around as long as I can remember," Nevan answered with indifference.

"You don't intend on giving him an answer?"

"I'm a Romalung, and Naoise is like a younger brother to me. He takes so much time and effort to look after that I can't take my eyes off him for a second. It's such a pain."

"I'm relieved to see you like him."

"Do not get the wrong idea."

I gave a strained laugh.

Nevan was genuinely concerned for Naoise, and she did love him, even if it wasn't in the romantic sense.

"Anyway, let us return. We need to write the demon subjugation report. With this, three demons have been defeated. At this rate, it seems like we'll have them all exterminated in no time," she said.

"You may be right. I hope the remaining ones aren't as strong as Liogel," I responded. Liogel had been ridiculously powerful. I didn't want to face anything like him again. "Tarte, Dia, let's go home. I'm starting to miss Tuatha Dé."

I decided I would leave the cleanup in Jombull to Nevan's subordinates. I could tell that they were skilled from watching them work for the past few days. I was sure they would deal with the situation nicely if I gave them loose instructions.

If you had talented personnel, you needed to make use of them.

"Yes, my lord. I'll make you your favorite Tuatha Dé food when we get back," said Tarte.

"Ooh, that sounds great!" exclaimed Dia.

"I will accompany you as well. I need to go ahead and introduce myself to your parents," added Nevan.

They were all behaving cheerfully for my sake, hoping to lift my spirits after my friend's departure.

It was kind of them. That's why I wanted to make sure I cherished the girls.

"Now, how should we get home? We're far from Jombull, and I doubt we could hire a carriage in the city's present state... How about we fly? There's no reason to hold back at this point. We could return to Tuatha Dé in less than half a day," I proposed.

Dia, Tarte, and Nevan exchanged a look, nodded, and responded together.

""""Sounds good, (my lord/Sir Lugh)!"""""

And thus, we decided to fly home. It would be a long trip, so I elected to produce a hang glider.

The weather was nice. Soaring through the pleasant blue sky seemed like as good a time as any to consider Naoise and what was to come next.

Afterword

Thank you very much for reading *The World's Finest Assassin Gets Reincarnated in Another World as an Aristocrat*, Vol. 4.

I am the author, Rui Tsukiyo.

Maha finally got the long-awaited spotlight this time.

Despite her limited appearances, she's very popular. That's why I gave her that scene. I like her as well, so I was happy to give her some attention.

This volume involved some new characters and featured the return of a certain handsome noble!

In the fifth volume, a threat separate from the demons will bare its fangs at Lugh. Please look forward to seeing how he handles it!

Promotion

This novel was released with a special version containing a drama CD! It features Kenji Akabane as Lugh, Reina Ueda as Dia, Yuuki Takada as Tarte, and Shino Shimoji as Maha! It's a star-studded cast.

I wrote the script specifically for the drama CD. It turned out twice as long as an average one, so you're more than getting your money's worth! Please give it a listen.

The manga for *The World's Finest Assassin Gets Reincarnated in Another World as an Aristocrat* series is available for purchase as well.

It's recently gotten an extra printing run, so you won't have any trouble finding it!

In other news, my new work published by MF Bunko J releases on April 25. The title is *Eiyuu Kyoushitsu No Chouetsu Majutsushi: Gendai Majutsu Wo Kiwameshimono, Tenseishite Tenshi Wo Shitagaeru*, and it's about a master of modern magic who achieves great success at a sorcery academy! He serves an angel, gets up to trouble with his younger sister-in-law, and strives to save a world on the brink of ruin.

The main character, Yuma, is just as cool and good-looking as Lugh. There's plenty more in the works for *The World's Finest Assassin Gets Reincarnated in Another World as an Aristocrat* series as well, so keep an eye out!

Thanks

Reia, thank you for providing wonderful illustrations for Volume 4. The special edition with the drama CD features more images than usual, but you made them all excellent!

To the editing team, all involved at Kadokawa Sneaker Bunko, lead designer Takahisa Atsuji, and all the people who have read this far, thank you very much!

The World's Finest Assassin Gets Reincarnated in Another World as an Aristocrat, Vol. 4

Congratulations on the release of Volume 4!!

Listen to the drama CD that comes out on the same day...
Listen to it...!!

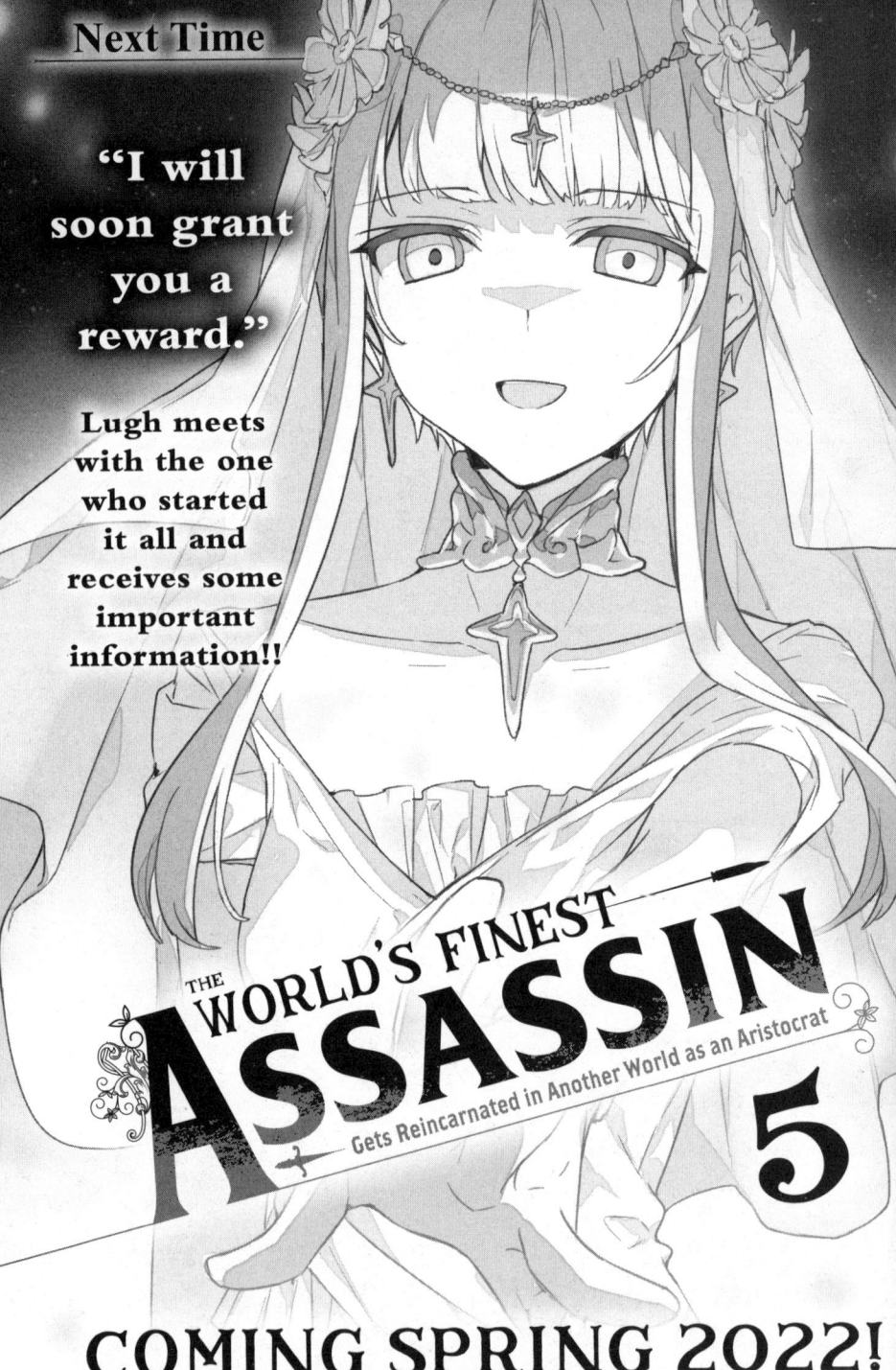